D1487356

An Accident of Love

An Accident of Love

a novel by

Mary Ellin Barrett

E. P. DUTTON & CO., INC. • NEW YORK

All the characters in this book are fictitious, and any resemblance to actual persons, living or dead, is purely coincidental.

Published simultaneously in Canada by
Clarke, Irwin & Company Limited, Toronto and Vancouver
Excerpts from this novel appeared
in *Ladies' Home Journal*, September 1973.

To my family, with gratitude

An Accident of Love

Chapter One

On the twentieth ring, the man stretched out on the sofa looked up at the woman and said, "Don't you think you should answer it?"

"I don't feel like answering it."

"It's very insistent. It might be important."

"I don't care. It's too late. It's too hot." Lightly, with long fingers, she traced his ears, his grizzled sideburns.

The phone stopped. Then, almost immediately, it began again. This time it kept ringing, twenty, thirty, forty times. Finally she slid out from under the man's big head, went into the bedroom, and picked up the receiver.

"Hello," she said, in her best telephone answering voice, prepared to tell whoever it was that she was out, in bed, in the hospital, in town, in Europe, or whatever fancy pleased her.

"I'd like to speak to Mrs. Browne, please." The voice was a man's, but pitched so low, and so hesitant in tone, that it was hard to tell whether the caller was young or old.

Mrs. Browne. For a moment she wondered who on earth that could be. Then she remembered and was not anxious to talk to the person asking for her. Some crank, no doubt, who had put name and number together.

"Hello. *Hello*. Mrs. Browne, please."

Ordinarily she would have hung up, but something in the voice held her. "Who is this?" she asked.

"Who is *this?*" said the voice, more sure of itself, even a little mocking. "Now let me speak to Mrs. Browne."

She didn't know the voice and yet she did. "I promise she'll want to talk to me," it continued. "But I want, see, I want to surprise her." A young person: that could be determined now. Very young, to have that voice and inflection.

"This is Mrs. Browne," she said harshly. "*Who are you?*"

"Hello, mother."

"Is this some sort of joke?"

"No joke. This is your son."

Silence. Absolute silence.

"Hello. Hello . . . are you there?"

"Yes, I'm here," she heard herself say. "I haven't fainted. How could I know your voice? I'd given up hearing from you a long time ago. For a minute I thought. I don't know what I thought. I'm slightly . . . what's taken you so *long*, you wretched boy. Where the hell are you?"

"In New York, mother. Home."

From the living room came another voice, the older, battered voice of the present. "Want something, Susan?"

He passed by the open door going toward the bar.

"No," she called. "Not yet. I'll be there in a minute." She pushed the door shut with her foot.

"Do you have guests, mother? Am I interrupting? Are you having a party?"

"No, Rick." At her neck the pulse had been a faint fluttering butterfly. Now it was a horse galloping home. She could barely speak.

"What do you look like?" he asked.

"I don't know. The same. A lot older, I guess. I don't have a mirror in front of me. You?"

"Not the same at all. Obviously. I used to look like you. I remember that. Now everyone says I'm the old man all over."

"Did you get my last letter, Rick?" Recovering now, she sounded sharper, brisker, more on the offensive.

"Yeah. I got it. They used to keep your letters from me. Then they let them through, but I didn't know what to answer. I was embarrassed."

"So now . . ."

"So now I'm twenty-one. A free man. And I think it's time I got to know my mother. Don't you think that'd be cool, for you and me to know each other?" Now the voice was spooky, really spooky. Through the surface dressing of today's style she could hear that other voice, so like it, so different. Then this one broke a little. "I want to *see* you."

I'm not going to cry, she said to herself. I gave that up years ago. I will not cry to this stranger who is my son. "When are you coming out, Rick?" she asked.

"Now."

"But there's no train this time of night."

"*Train?* I've got a car, mother. I'm a big boy. How long does it take?"

"Two and a half, three hours, depending on the traffic."

"I'll make it in two." He laughed. She liked his laugh. It was warm. It broke over her. She wondered what he looked like when he laughed. "Don't worry, mother, I'm a good driver. If *you* give me good directions."

"Got a pencil?" As she talked she saw herself sitting, not on the side of her bed holding onto the phone, but in a car beside a laughing young man, holding onto his knee, feeling scared as they streaked through the night along that same route she was defining, long before the new expressways.

"Maybe you should wait till morning," she said to the son of that young man now.

"Relax, mother. I'll be there. About one."

"Rick. Drive carefully. *Rick.*"

But he was gone.

She hung up the receiver and went into the living room, a glass and steel prism thrusting out into dark woods beside a lapping pond. It was warm that late May night, the air a heavy moist substance you could touch but scarcely breathe. The first bugs were crawling through the hole in one of the sliding screens she had meant to have fixed weeks earlier.

"Who was that?" asked the man who was once more stretched out on the sofa, drinking a scotch and smoking one of his vile cigars. "You look terribly upset." The sea gray eyes watching her were tired and quizzical.

"God, it's stuffy." Ignoring the question, she sat on the loveseat opposite him.

"Why don't we go outside?"

"We'll get eaten alive. How about putting out that thing?"

"No," clamping the cigar in his teeth, standing up. "No, I won't put it out." Unwinding the great length of him, he towered above her. "Now tell me who that was?"

"That was my son."

A pause. A frown. After a final puff of smoke, he crushed out the cigar.

"I didn't know about a son."

"Neither did I." She was looking at his glass. "I think if I had a drink now it wouldn't make any difference. It might help."

"No," the man said. "I'll get you some coffee. Have a cigarette. Forget about giving up smoking."

"How old is he?" the man asked. He handed her a mug of coffee along with a cigarette and sat beside her. She had to let him sit there because if she cut him off, what else did she have?

"He's twenty-one. His birthday was a few months ago. I wrote him a letter. I guess he got it. He's been living in England."

"How long since you've seen him?"

She sat quite motionless.

"Can you talk about it? Can you talk about anything to do with yourself?"

"Can you?"

"We're not talking about me. I could tell you I don't believe you have a twenty-one-year-old son but that would be a lie."

She was mildly amused. "Considering I was thirty-three when I had him, it certainly would," she said. "You'll have to do better than that."

"You're giving me a lot of precious statistics." He took her hand. She dug her nails into his palm.

"You've never mentioned a son, or a husband, for that matter," the man said. "Everyone around here assumes you have some sort of past and don't want to talk about it. *Susan Rose*. It sounds made up, a pen name."

"It is, and it isn't."

"What's the boy's name?"

"Michael. Michael Richards. Though we called him Rick."

"Richards the last name?"

"No. The middle name."

"Michael Richards what?"

She hesitated. "Michael Richards Browne," she said finally.

There was a long silence. Then the man said, quite flatly, "It's all right. I guessed. Long ago. You're Susannah Browne."

("You're not Susan," the boy's father had said the day they met. "Susan is a lousy name for you. I'm going to call you

Susannah." And rechristened her with a bottle of wedding champagne.)

"That's right. Why didn't you say anything?"

"I was waiting for you to tell me. And that's Mike Browne's son."

"Yes."

"You poor woman," he said.

She hated the look on his face and wanted to wipe it off with her bare palms. She wanted to assure him that before the end was a beginning; before she was a woman to be pitied, avoided, even feared, she was a woman to be envied and courted, a creature most blessed. She wanted to tell him something else, too: about the wedding. The picture of the wedding. The people in the picture. But that was the part of the story that went past melodrama, sensationalism, past a dozen people's lives into something ghastly and inexplicable—something she, a writer, could never have grasped or dared imagine. But maybe he, the man with the cigar, could. He was a great one for answers and explanations.

Part I

Chapter Two

They met at a wedding, an ordinary enough way for a girl to meet the boy she is going to marry, except this was not quite an ordinary wedding, nor ordinary the presence there of a girl named Susan Rose, nor ordinary by any stretch of the imagination her effect on the boy, Michael Richards Browne. Certainly everyone could see why he wanted to take her out and dance with her and screw her and buy her diamonds, because in her own way she was quite an object. As his Uncle James, the family joker, said to him over cigars and brandy one night, "I wish I'd had a swell piece o'tail like that tuh cut muh teeth on!" But *marry* her. People even questioned that she'd been at the wedding at all, preferring the columnists' version, a mixing of several stories, that the prince had picked up Cinderella on the Stork Club dance floor.

But there she was, mainly because the bride, Kitty St. John, the most beautiful girl in New York, wanted to teach the groom, Red Jones, the recently returned navy hero, a lesson. He needed a few lessons, that boy. John Edgar Jones was full of spunk, full of himself, full (as Susan's old Uncle Dan, her family's joker, would have put it) of prune whip. And full of little tricks to make a girl squirm like a fish on a hook and moan with frustration.

Kitty and Susan had made friends during the autumn of 1945, in the offices of the fashion magazine where they both worked, because Kitty was furious at Red and needed someone to talk to and Susan happened to be passing by.

Ordinarily their paths would not have crossed. Kitty St. John was an assistant to Elena Worden, the fashion editor, a lady noted for hiring as apprentices pretty debutantes rather than ambitious and brainy college graduates. Girls one knew, those were the ones Elena (herself a Newport Devreaux) preferred; "Girls," she said, "who cheer me up to look at." Susan Rose was the assistant literary editor, clearly brainy, plainly ambitious, most definitely not a debutante and not anyone to cheer up Elena Worden. "Loud" was the adjective most frequently applied to Susan Rose, though a few called her lovely and later, when she was considered one of the most attractive women in New York, these few could say: we told you so.

Susan Rose had wavy blue black hair that glistened like dragonfly wings and cascaded over her shoulders. She had coffee ice cream skin and cheeks so unusually pink for that kind of olive complexion that everyone thought she wore rouge, and she stared at you with big hazel eyes, so heavily lashed everyone thought they were false. Her mouth was curious—attractively so—with a full lower lip and a thin upper. Her nose was slightly beaked and her figure was the sort that elicited whistles from truck drivers, construction workers, school boys and all manner of men, and merciless comments from other women. Men and women alike spoke of her appearance as Spanish, Italian, Egyptian, Mexican, Latin, Mediterranean, everything except Jewish, which in fact she looked and was. Mrs. Worden pronounced judgment on Susan: "Overblown, that young woman, overpainted and overperfumed. Like the last Rose of summer."

Known around the office respectively as The Last Word and The Last Rose, Elena and Susan detested each other, and Susan did her best to avoid the offices of the fashion department. But that particular day she happened by in search of a stray piece of copy and came upon a glorious blonde, Miss Kitty St. John, sitting at her desk sobbing, throwing crumpled papers at the wall separating the outer cubicle from The Last Word's pink and purple bower within. Susan felt sorry for the latest bit of fluff reduced to tears by her boss's notoriously sharp tongue and spoke to the girl.

"It's not *her*," Kitty said. "I've got her number. What woman ever made you cry?" She had a whispering, utterly charming voice with a bit of a lisp, the "r's" melting into "w's." "It's this stupid boy. I don't *like* him, but I'm *crazy* about him. You know what he did . . . ?"

Susan found herself listening. She was after all a writer and writers were trained to listen. Before too long she had laughed the girl out of it, telling a sad story of her own, explaining that all men were perfect bastards and what could you do? Later that week they had lunch. Over cottage cheese and fruit (both were on the latest nine-day diet craze, though Susan couldn't see why Kitty was; she was slim as a Shakespearean boy-girl) they told each other rather personal things—as new acquaintances sometimes do in a certain mood—and thus became friends, sharing a mocking way of looking at life and a passionate concern with men. They would never get truly close because they were unfamiliar to each other, the debutante and the writer, the fashionable East-sider and the bright Jewish girl from Riverside Drive, but they liked each other. Each was the other's special, interesting friend.

So what else should Kitty have done, when Red Jones said to her after meeting Susan Rose one Friday evening at the Stork Club, "Where'd you dig that one up, princess? What the *hell* is that?" What else but say, "*That* is my friend Susan Rose, kiddo! *That* is one of my bridesmaids!" There wasn't a blessed thing Red or his mother, Mrs. Stuyvesant Jones, the super dreadnought of New York society, or Kitty's mother, Mrs. Purvis St. John, known among Kitty's friends as Mrs. Perfection, could do except deplore this new age in which a well brought up girl like Kitty St. John could take up at work with a *person* like Susan Rose. And not just take up, but invite her to be a member of her wedding.

Afterward, when Mrs. Stuyvesant Jones had retired to Palm Beach and Mrs. Purvis St. John to London and young Mrs. Michael Browne was turning the town on its ear, Red Jones forgot that he'd ever felt anything but immediate liking for Kitty's offbeat friend. "I always had my eye on you, Susie," he'd say (ignoring the fact that she detested being so called) and would serenade her with "If You Knew Susie," Eddie Cantor style. But Susan would remember otherwise.

The Stork Club was jammed, the columnists on the prowl. In the Cub Room, the inner sanctum, movie stars and theater people sat around gossiping, while out front college boys and debutantes and out-of-town suckers danced to the whistling, clattering South American band. Among the dancers was Susan Rose, there, as she often was that winter, in the company of Bill Wolfe, a clever young *Time* writer with lank black hair and circles under his eyes who wanted very much to marry her.

They had come out of the Cub Room where they always sat (thanks to a friendly story he'd written on the night club's proprietor) and were moving expertly around the floor, knowing they were better than anyone else there. A few seasons later, Mike Browne, who was worth millions but couldn't dance worth a dime, would pull his wife off the floor for showing off like that with a man. But single, she could do as she pleased and enjoy the fact that people stared at her, taking in her splendid legs, her whole voluptuous person encased in a lamé dancing dress. As happened from time to time, a smart-alec golden boy winked at her from a floorside table, rose to his feet and tried to cut in. She secretly liked that and liked the way Bill Wolfe handled the boy, with a quick joke, so that he laughed and went away instead of making trouble as such boys when drunk often do. "Some nights going out wiith you is like going out with a pot of honey. Too damn many flies," Bill said to her, holding her close for a moment before spinning her around.

That night, she thought it might be a lot of fun being Mrs. Bill Wolfe, with an apartment in the East Fifties, a rowdy group of reporter friends, a bright-eyed little baby crawling around and a nanny so she could keep her job, work on her novel and still go with Bill to all the screenings and openings. Later they'd move to Hollywood, because that was where Bill was bound to end up, making his own movies instead of writing about them. They'd be famous. She smiled at him. Hers was not the dazzling sort, but rather a sweet smile, in the shape of a sickle moon, scarcely showing her teeth, which were small, even, like pearls of white corn. A smile with a mysterious green light in it. *Go.*

Then she saw the others come in.

She saw a whole group of them in evening clothes, those glittering girls just grown up and those brassy boys just back from the war that Elena Worden called "the Squad" and was forever photographing and writing about. Long before they became the Jet Set or the Browne set or the Beautiful People, they were Elena's Squad; or more simply "They"—the dazzling young ones who set the styles, who were always the first at a new place, first with the new fad. "They" were the ones with pedigreed names and unlimited money who, unlike the generation before, spent conspicuously without regard to taste or appearances. "They" were the party-goers and brawlers whose stupendous good looks and monumental bad behavior dazzled and terrified everyone.

As if on cue, the rhumba band gave way to the fox trot orchestra, which played their song, a song written some years earlier but one that mirrored this postwar time, the song Kitty was always singing: . . . *it was great fun but it was just one of those things*. Susan Rose thought it a fatuous song. She'd had one of those crazy things, but they didn't meet now and then, and it was no fun. But the Squad smiled, snapping their fingers, dancing little steps, getting in the mood as they moved past the velvet rope behind which others had been waiting for an hour. Laughing loudly, waving, stopping to say hello, they moved noisily and conspicuously to the special tables that had just been set up for them directly on the dance floor, making it even smaller than it already was.

From pictures, Susan recognized a number of them: Big Jack Weatherby, the former all-American and his auburn-haired wife Diana, rawboned, disheveled, always looking as if she'd been blown in by a hurricane; Mimi Bryan, the society songbird with robin bright eyes and feathery platinum hair; Anthony George, the gossip columnist with guardsman's mustache and eyes that fastened on you like ticks, whose grandmother had been an English duchess; Georgie von Groot, the accordion-playing playgirl; Clark "Larky" Harrison, ex-navy, the polo-playing playboy; Pete Plainfield, heir to a copper fortune, married to the highest paid model in the world; Jimmy Parr, the young stockbroker just out of the marines whose father owned half of New York, and his wife Christine, tiny, snooty as a peacock, and the greatest heiress on the eastern seaboard; Charlie Clay, who was salt, and his wife Patsy, who was Ham; Sasha Garden, the mysterious businessman, new on the scene, who, disliking publicity, had threatened to withdraw advertising (he had a controlling interest in several textile houses) from the magazine when Elena printed a party snap of him; and at their center, flame to the lunar moths, moved Kitty St. John, with floating yellow hair and turquoise eyes and a ruby lipped smile. Holding Kitty's arm was a tall boy with short-cropped red hair, a captivating jack-o'-lantern grin, a strut like a gob dancer in a wartime musical, her fiancé, the devastating Mr. Jones.

Susan Rose hated them all, scorned and mocked them in her heart. Yet, watching them, she suddenly and ignobly wished she were part of them because they seemed to be having so much more fun, because they seemed to know some secret, or own some key to the pleasures of the earth, because they would always be the rope-jumpers and the line-crashers, the ones to go first. From the dance floor Susan waved to Kitty.

Presently the two girls and their captive men stood at the edge, an awkward foursome making awkward conversation. Susan told Kitty a bit of gossip she knew would amuse her friend, but Red Jones didn't laugh and looked suddenly weary. "Come join us," Kitty said to Susan. "I want you to meet everyone." Red's mouth, not his best feature when closed, pursed. His eyebrows lowered in a petty frown. He turned toward the tables, shouting something, and someone shouted back, "Eh, Jonesie, eh boy, you tell 'em."

"You know Lily and Luis and the Taylors are coming, too," Red said to Kitty. "It's going to be sardines."

"Pooh." She made a little *moue*.

"Thanks," said Bill Wolfe, "it looks crowded."

"Some other time," said Susan. "Give us a rain check."

They returned to the Cub Room, which now seemed to Susan dull and middle-aged. "Will you *stop that*," she said suddenly, very loudly, to Bill Wolfe who was chewing on a wooden match. "*Please.*"

"Don't take it out on me, kid," he said.

A few days later, Kitty told Susan she was going to be married in May and asked her to be a bridesmaid. Knowing the character of her friend, remembering the look on the fiancé's face, Susan sensed the origin of the invitation and could imagine the exchange between the lovers as clearly as if she had heard it. (Later when Kitty, angry at Red, recounted the whole conversation, Susan laughed and teased her friend: "I knew.") But it didn't matter. She was tired of nervous journalists like Bill Wolfe who thought they owned her; of the lavender lanes of Upper Bohemia; of Second Avenue walk-ups and Greenwich Village bars and Brooklyn Heights salons; of scrounging; of herself, Susan Rose, born Susannah Rosoff, scholarship girl, clever editor, writer of precocious stories for *Mademoiselle* and the *Bazaar*. She wanted a look at Kitty's world, even if the groom did seem like a stuffed shirt.

Chapter Three

As it turned out, of course, there were no bridesmaids at the St. John-Jones wedding. It wasn't that sort of affair, which made a stranger's presence even more conspicuous. In the *Times* the next day, Kitty's picture was the largest on the page. The account took up three columns to accommodate all the distinguished forebears of two such wealthy and conspicuous families. But the wedding was small and simple, taking place, both ceremony and reception, at the St. John house on Ninetieth Street. Just forty people in a bricked-in city garden blooming with magnolias and tulips, the immediate families and the bride and groom's closest friends, the ones who would have been ushers and bridesmaids.

All the elaborate plans had been canceled—the bridal dinner, the ceremony at St. James, the River Club reception, and most of the parties—since six weeks earlier Purvis St. John had been killed, tragically, in a riding accident. Gloria St. John was in mourning and so there was no question, under the circumstances, of a big wedding. Aside from anything else, Gloria couldn't manage without Purvy and that was that.

"The Joneses are furious," Kitty said to Susan over a last lunch the week she left the office. "Mother's so funny about some things. In mourning nowadays. If the truth were known, I understood Pops better than she did. He would have wanted me to have my big wedding. He would have hated us in black." For her daughter's wedding, however, Gloria had put away her widow's weeds and wore gray silk and a feathered hat, looking exactly as Susan had long ago imagined a society lady would look. She was a lovely woman, Mrs. Perfection, a brunette version of her daughter. It was from her mother that Kitty had her eyes and her cheekbones and her widow's peak. From her mother, too, Kitty had inherited her lisping, whispering voice and the shape of her smile; only Gloria's voice croaked from too many cigarettes, and her smile came from the head, Kitty's from the heart.

"So very pleased to meet you," Gloria said to Susan Rose, greeting her at the door. "Kitty's often spoken about you." Gloria switched on a smile of perhaps 40-watt brightness. She led her toward a group of guests in the garden and placed her between a rattled old lady and a scowling young man, introduced as Kitty's grandmother and Gus Gladstone, a friend of the groom. Recognition. Amusement. Gus was the boy who had tried to cut in on Susan at the Stork Club.

"Hi," he said, giving her his insolent wink. "Small world. We'll have a dance yet."

But Susan Rose would have only one dance that wedding day, with Mike Browne, the best man.

She saw him first standing beside Red Jones, holding the ring. Two things struck her: his beautiful sullen profile and his poor posture.

Much later he told her that he had first caught a scarlet flash of her standing among the other guests on the right side of the garden door, as he walked with the groom to the far end where the minister stood.

During the service, he said, he had wanted to turn and take a good look, but stood stiffly at attention, eyes forward. All his life he had been awkward and ill at ease with formality and ceremonies. After four years in the army he had been away too long from such occasions and was genuinely afraid that if he moved he would do something wrong, drop the ring or begin to sneeze, or laugh. But most of all he was afraid that when the minister said, "Does anyone know of any reason why these two should not . . ." a voice not his own would thunder forth from his mouth, "Yeah, I do." No such thing happened. John Edgar Jones and Katherine Alice St. John, young, irresponsible, and totally unprepared, who never in any sane world should have married, were man and wife, kissing and laughing, their white smiles seeming to split their handsome faces in half.

Then they were kissing and hugging everyone: the reverend and his wife, who wore a pigeon for a hat; Mrs. St. John; Kitty's cousin Jay Lawrence, beautiful like all the family but pale and faintly yellow, his hair, teeth and skin like ivory; Red's parents, a Myrna Loy mother, a Thomas Dewey father; Red's much younger sister Natalie, known as P.S., a pudgy eight-year-old with straw hair and glasses, looking as though she'd be happier in blue jeans than the candy pink party dress she had on; the grannies, one a Jones, one a St. John, who had been bridesmaids at each other's weddings fifty years earlier. There were two other twin ladies, identified as the nannies, his and hers, who claimed that the bride and groom had met first not at a cocktail party but in Central Park. The uncle who had given Kitty away looked like a bear. An aunt looked like a toucan. There was a man who resembled a hard-boiled egg, and a trio—mommy and daddy, and grown-up son, large, perspiring, and red-faced—who looked like horses and who, Susan learned later at lunch, came from the deep riding country of New Jersey. There was a melancholy lady with a long face like a sugared almond, who fingered her rouged cheeks and said, "But they are so young. Were we ever that young?"

The older people collected their hugs and kisses and then they gave way to the friends, the young men in smart pin-striped suits and the girls in their spring dresses. Everyone was joking, teasing, kissing, blowing smoke, waving glasses of champagne, and somewhere in that crowding and kissing and waving, Mike Browne bumped into Susan Rose and spilled his champagne down the front of her dress.

"Hey," he said, "you should look where you're going."

"*I* should look where *I'm* going?"

"Yeah, well, it's hard to see where you're going some days, especially if you're not quite all there."

"I beg your pardon," she said, looking into two sleepy blood-shot blue eyes, deciding he was crazy but grateful nonetheless to be spoken to by someone.

"You looked the way I feel. As if you wanted out of here." His voice was deep, nasal, lazy, but not quite the standard prep school accent that pronounces car "core," God "gawd," and tacks an "*r*" onto all words ending in "*a*." There was something harder, more roughshod about it. A voice that had gone down in the world a bit and profited thereby. An extremely attractive voice, instantly personal, like his stare.

"It's that I don't know anyone."

"Christ, I *am* sorry, really."

"That's all right," she said. "It'll dry." Of her voice, he said later, "New Yorkese, a real gutter voice that's come up in the world."

"How about some salt?" he said.

"That's for red wine."

"Well, sugar? Sugar would help all the way around."

"*Honestly*. Listen, what's your name?"

"Mike Browne." The eyes were amused, unembarrassed and

they were, bloodshot or not, the bluest eyes she'd ever seen.

"I'm Susan Rose."

"Whose friend are you?" he asked, continuing to examine her, speculatively, almost insolently.

"The bride's," Kitty said, coming up to them. "This is *Susan Rose,*" which didn't mean a thing to Mike Browne, but the face and the shape, those meant something. "I keep forgetting, Brownie," Kitty went on, twitching her nose at him, "you don't read anything but the stupid papers and you don't listen to anything I tell you, and what have you done to my friend? This one never looks where he's going," she said to Susan. "The other night we were walking down Park Avenue together and coming out of the Waldorf . . ."

"The Ambassador," he corrected.

"All right, the Ambassador, well, coming out of *some* hotel was a man carrying a great pyramid of packages. I didn't recognize him . . ."

"Because you're blind."

"Stop interrupting. I did not recognize him but . . ."

They laughed and contradicted each other and Susan laughed too, but she couldn't quite tell what it was all about: who the distinguished package carrying head of state was, what ridiculous thing Mike Browne had done. She only pretended to listen, using intent interest in what he was saying as an excuse to look at him.

Except for those half-buried hungover eyes, he was without question the best looking young man she had ever seen—spectacularly handsome—in an old-fashioned way. He was of medium height, perhaps three inches taller than she, but in the spike heels she wore that day (and every day till he told her he hated them) they were about the same. He had thick dark brown hair parted neither on the side nor in the middle but somewhere between the two. One lock of it flopped heavily over his forehead. He had a chiseled nose that fell straight from his smooth brow, a sullen sensuous mouth, a well-defined cleft chin and eyebrows like dark wings. She wouldn't have said he resembled Laurence Olivier, an actor who turned her bones to jelly, but still he could have played Heathcliffe or Darcy.

Presently Kitty moved on to another group, seeing her friend was set, for a while anyhow.

"So tell me about yourself, Susan Rose." He seemed to find something comical about the name. "The bride gives me the impression that I should know who you are." He grinned. Unlike his nose, his teeth, she noticed, weren't quite straight, but the smile was unbelievable—of the big open American variety—as homey as apple pie, as sneaky as a first kiss. The smile and the eyes went together. "Frankly, I don't have a clue. I've been away for a long while. I don't know who anybody is."

"Including Mike Browne, I'll bet."

"Outta the way there, outta the way, Brownie, boh." It was beat-up Gus Gladstone, balancing a tray of champagne like a musical comedy waiter, introduced to her again.

"We've met," Susan said. Short, blonde, scowling, he looked, she decided, like a Pekingese. The nighttime dinner jacketed golden boy had vanished. Already he was very drunk. Susan and her friends drank a lot, but they never got drunk. He mumbled something to Mike Browne. Mike laughed heartily, taking two glasses off the tray and handing one to Susan. The tray teetered, the glasses slopped.

"Watch-t . . . watch-t there, Brownie-boh, watch wat-r-doin', boh," said Gus. He squinted at Susan. "She wouldn't dance with me. Stuck up."

"We hadn't been introduced. I'd dance with you now."

"No, you wou'n't. Still stuck up. Like muh wife. Ya r'mind me of muh wife. Don' think, Brownie, boh? When you an' me first picked up the babe?"

"What the hell are you talking about, Gladstone?"

"History, dear boh, *re*peats." Giving a rather crooked smile, he moved on. "Watch-t, Mrs. J," Susan heard him say, "Watch-t, reverend."

"Where'd *you* meet that character?" asked Mike Browne, already assuming the protector's role.

"He tried to pick me up one night in the Stork Club. I certainly wouldn't have guessed he was married."

"He's not, most days. You're not the least like his wife except she has a lot of black curly hair. Over there . . ." He pointed to a striking dark girl in yellow, talking with her hands, catching sunlight on her bracelets. "He met her at a canteen in London, under my care. Dominique Dumaine." He pronounced it with heavy comic accent, shaking his head. "A would-be starlet touring with some USO troupe. She calls herself Dolly."

"She's pretty. A few too many rhinestones. But pretty."

"Those aren't rhinestones, baby, those are the real thing. That's Dolly's problem. On her, nothing looks real. Well, you know what they say about USO girls . . ."

"I worked for the USO for a while."

"You know what I mean."

"No, I don't." She could feel the prick of indignation, a sympathy for dismissed Dolly. But then again he gave her that impossible grin and what could she do but return it.

"A girl who knows her own mind, I can see that. You realize I've ruined you," he said, staring at the drying stain, which had left a large and conspicuous ring covering the bosom of her dress. A mistake, that dress. American beauty red raw silk, with glittering buttons that, like Dolly Gladstone's bracelets, caught the sun. Until today she had liked it. Now she saw it was all wrong for a morning wedding. She also had the uncomfortable feeling that under her arms another sort of stain had formed. She should have worn a different, darker dress, should have known that on such an occasion her nerves would go straight to her armpits.

"Here," he said, reaching over to Gloria St. John's prize magnolia tree, plucking off one blossom, then another, sticking the stems through a buttonhole. Where his fingers touched, it was as if she'd been singed by a hot iron. "There, that hides it a bit." Where his eyes rested, it was as if she'd been hit by a ray of sun through a magnifying glass.

"Look at Kitty," she said, wanting to move those eyes off her. "Look how beautiful she is."

The bride was standing in the curve of the brick wall, her arm in the groom's, smiling for the photographer. She was visibly tipsy and she had taken off her veil, loose hair blowing in the breeze. Of all the golden girls in the world, she was the most golden.

"Girls always are on their wedding day. So will you be. Or were you?"

"I'm not married."

"Girls are always what on their wedding day?" A smooth-haired, narrow-faced young man, scornful of manner, beautiful of dress, immediately recognizable as Pete Plainfield, the young sportsman, had stopped to speak to Mike Browne, though he seemed to be looking past him, looking for someone else. With Plainfield was a bony windblown redhead, dressed in puritan gray, also recognizable to Susan as Diana Weatherby, leader of the fashionable young marrieds, proof a plain girl could get around.

"Pregnant, Pete, what else?"

"Smashed," said Diana. "And can you blame us? Think what we're signing away." They went on a bit, as if Susan weren't there, till Mike made the introductions.

"I know who you are," said Peter Plainfield. "You write. My wife is crazy about your stories. I don't read, otherwise I'm sure I'd be crazy about them, too. I'm going to go find her." He disappeared and didn't return, which was the way of young men who know the art of spreading themselves thin.

"Where's Lily?" Diana Weatherby asked Mike Browne. "I need to see her in the worst possible way."

"How should I know where Lily is."

"I thought you knew her every move, Brownie, twenty-four hours a day." Her tone was teasing, proprietary, that of an old friend; her voice as deep as a boy's and oddly sexy coming from such a gawky girl.

"Me and all New York." He seemed to have forgotten Susan Rose. "What are you two up to?"

"Mischief. . . . Yay, there she is," a big grin spreading over her freckled face. "Hey Lil, where have you been?" she shouted through cupped hands.

The girl came out of the house and waved back, gesturing extravagantly, in the direction of Mike Browne and Di Weatherby. She was a dish, this one, with a showgirl's hourglass figure poured into a tight and gaudy silk print, a dress that on anyone else would have been dismissed as cheap. On Susan Rose, say, such a dress would *not do*. But on Lily Welles, the dress was simply a background for masses of expensive gold jewelry, a stem for an incredible blooming of dark blonde hair that hung thick and shining in a pageboy bob around a pretty pouting, painted face. A study for the year 1946, that was Lily Welles.

Mike Browne made a small gesture in response to her wave, a curiously personal gesture, as if they needed no shouts, no big hello's, but he made no move to leave Susan Rose and go toward her. It was her girl friend, Di Weatherby, who walked to her and began whispering to her with female urgency and muffled laughter, imparting whatever information was so pressing. "God, Di, O.K.," Lily Welles said, purring like an icebox. "Now help me find Mrs. Saint. She's going to kill me. Come on, you can make it all right. Make her laugh the way you always do."

"Who are *they*?" Susan Rose asked Mike Browne.

"Lily Welles and Di Weatherby. The ones we're all crazy about. The great girls."

"Hmmph . . ." Susan Rose made a small exact noise.

At lunch they sat at separate tables. On Susan's right was a dark-haired, bull-necked man, Diana's husband, big Jack Weatherby, who talked through the entire lunch in the same slurry muffled tones as Gus Gladstone, to blonde Carol Plainfield on his other side. On Susan's left sat the amiable and red-faced cousin who looked like a horse, Willis Metcalf. She tried unsuccessfully to break into the conversation on her right and to introduce herself to the assured blonde, whose eyes were hidden behind sapphire sunglasses, who was said to read her stories. "Your husband says . . ." she began three times, then gave up and allowed herself to be appropriated by cousin Willis who was noisy and extremely friendly. He told her all about fox hunting and cock fighting and kept putting his hand on her knee, till his mother having X-ray vision (how else could she see under the table?) said, "Willy, you'll ruin that young lady's dress with those sticky hands of yours. You're drunk as a lord." As was she. Across the bright airy dining room, done in exquisite Chinese wallpaper with flying birds and bending grass, Mike Browne sat between the bride and the bewitching maid of honor, Mimi Bryan. He seemed enchanted with his place, except from time to time he would catch the eye of the dark and earthy Susan Rose.

Immediately after the cake and the singing and the toasts, when everyone had begun dancing in the next room to a piano and implacably jaunty violin, Mike Browne disappeared and Susan was sure he had left. He was the sort, she sensed, who'd cut out fast from this kind of affair. Still she wondered why he hadn't at least said good-by and felt so let down that she began to wonder when she could politely leave. The music seemed flat, so she went into the garden, where she found him playing catch with Natalie Jones, Red's little sister. The girl threw like a boy. Susan watched them until the child suddenly noticed her and ran back into the house. "I didn't mean to scare her away," she said.

"You didn't. That kid doesn't scare. Poor thing. She was going crazy in there, downing champagne like coke." He sat down on a stone bench, still bouncing the ball.

"I thought you'd gone," she said, wishing immediately she hadn't. He raised his eyebrows slightly and instead of speaking simply tossed her the ball, which she missed. "Butterfingers," he said, "ten of them. Pick it up."

"*No.*" She sat beside him on the bench and they talked together for a while. As they talked, she had the curious sensation of having always known him, this boy she couldn't possibly begin to know, which of course was not at all curious; it was the first and most ordinary symptom of falling in love.

"Susan," he said after a while, "is a lousy name for you. You're not a Susan."

"No?"

"Susan is a red-haired bitch with no front."

"My real name is Susannah."

"That's more like it. That goes with you."

"I always hated that name. It sounds so old-fashioned. I got teased a lot."

"Susannah makes me think of the one with the elders. Someone to spy on. Some gorgeous biblical broad with black hair and olive eyes. You shouldn't have changed it, Susannah. If there's one thing I can't stand it's a Jew who changes her name."

"Really?"

"Joke," he said. "Bad joke," catching something in her face, misinterpreting amusement for indignation.

"No joke," she said. "Guess what?"

"Oh," he said.

"You know," he said, "for a Jew to get in here is like a rich man getting into heaven." And that, for a while anyhow, took care of that.

"I'm going to christen you Susannah," he said, flicking champagne on her hair. "Tell me some more about yourself, bright girl. Where do you come from? What do you do besides work on a magazine and write stories? I want to know everything about you."

"I doubt you could take it. I think you'd be too shocked."

"I've taken it so far."

"Some other time."

"I won't beg you. You'll tell me sooner or later more than I want to hear. Girls always do." So indeed she did, and not all that much later, until finally he said, "Enough. Save it for your novel. As far as I'm concerned you were born around twelve noon on a May Saturday in nineteen forty-six, in a garden on East Ninetieth."

But that day she didn't want to talk. She wanted to listen and unearth the man beneath the tag that read: *Veteran; not back long; handle with care. Breakable.*

"I'd rather hear about you," she said. "Where were you in the war?"

"Europe. Up the boot, France and Germany."

"I'd have thought you were navy. Most boys like you were."

"I'd have thought a girl like you wouldn't make a generalization like that."

"What are your plans?"

The question seemed to annoy him. "To raise hell. Have the greatest time anybody ever had. Christ, how do I know what I'm going to do?" he added abruptly. "Take some job away from some woman, maybe? Why don't you go and pick up that ball."

"O.K.," she said lightly, she who never humored anyone, picking the ball out of the shrubbery, tossing it back to him, an impossible toss he caught. Then he pitched the ball hard, high over the brick wall into the street, looking out past the houses across the way to the city spires beyond, blue and gleaming in the afternoon light. Watching him she remembered something Kitty had said about Mike Browne: "a work of art but an idiot."

"Is your girl giving you a bad time? Is that why you're so cross?"

"What girl?"

"The sexy blonde. She has to be your girl."

"She's everybody's property. I don't have a girl. These girls don't like me. They think I'm . . . uncouth. You've got a chance, Susannah." Now he was grinning again, teasing. He was, no question, gorgeous. Stupid girls.

"Do I? Wonderful! I can see you're a real bargain."

"Oh, but I am, bright girl," he said, standing up, pulling her up beside him. "Did you know I was very rich? Did you know I'm a catch? The daughters may not know it, but their mothers sure as hell do."

"No," she said. At that moment it clicked. Now she could see the name in print. Not Brown. Browne. Those ones. The Brownes-with-an-e. Browne Center, Browne Pavilion, the Browne wing of the Metropolitan. Browne Lake in the Adirondacks. Camp Browne, the famous family compound. She could see the name: on plaques, in the society columns, in listings of trustees and board members of every cultural and philanthropic organization in the city. But not till that moment. That was the truth.

Some people were standing in the garden door now, looking out, looking at them. From the house came the sound of feet shuffling, of fast music, the piano thumping, the violin swinging. It was the moment at any dancing party when the band begins a medley of "Alexander's Ragtime Band," "Tiger Rag," "Twelfth Street Rag," "Darktown Strutters Ball," the moment just before they play the slow songs that signal the party's end. Susannah could feel her feet beginning to move.

"Don't you want to dance?" she asked, since he obviously wasn't going to ask her.

"I'm terrible."

"I'm not."

"You will be with me. You wait. But what the hell. Let's give it a try."

Terrible was an understatement. He couldn't keep time and moved, for someone so obviously a marvelous athlete, in a surprisingly clumsy way, putting his feet and long legs where she least expected him to. He clowned. He bent her back. He went suddenly limp and she stumbled. He made her think of the toy brought to her when she was little by her slightly rich Uncle Dan Rubinstein, her mother's brother, who always came up for her birthday from Miami, where he had a clothing store. Every year Dan arrived, bringing splendor to the gloomy Riverside Drive apartment, cracking jokes and showering his favorite niece with gifts. The day she was nine he gave her a stuffed doll as tall as she was, all long arms and legs and floppy hands and feet. When she danced with it, its arms would sag around her neck, its legs would bend around hers.

"That's it, captain," someone shouted as she struggled now. "Strut your stuff, sir, show them how they taught you at Arthur Murray's."

"Cut," said Jay Lawrence, ivory cousin of the golden bride. "This girl deserves a break."

"No cut," said Mike Browne. "Beat it, Lawrence."

Then, mercifully, the music slowed down to a waltz, the slowest saddest waltz in the world, the one they always play at weddings. Red and Kitty came onto the floor for a last dance before it was time for her to change her dress.

"I don't want to leave this party," Susan heard her say to Red. Her voice was fuzzy, the lisp acute. "It's the best party I've ever had." He whispered something in her ear and she laughed and said, "All right, Jonesie, all *right,*" pronouncing "right" like "white."

Kitty's cousin Jay was with little Natalie Jones, pushing her around the floor like a vacuum cleaner. You could tell at a glance that Jay Lawrence, the group dandy, was also the one who would be nice to younger sisters and country cousins, who'd snarl under his breath but come through with the good deed. (Indeed, a minute later he took the kid to the powder room to be sick.) Gus Gladstone was with Carol Plainfield, his dog's eyes happily closed; Peter Plainfield was with the seductive Lily, eyes only half closed, not talking, holding her close, each announcing their roles: prowlers, death on the opposite sex. The Weatherbys were dancing together, double-time, their arms held high in that strange lock favored by such types, their heads thrown back, the sort of people, Susannah sensed, who would always move twice as fast as anyone else. On the side, not dancing, was a rollicking trio, Dolly Gladstone, Willis Metcalf, and Mimi Bryan, Willis with his arms around both girls. Dolly's eyes were fixed on her husband, Mimi's on her best friend Kitty, as if forcing a blessing on her, demanding she be happy. Suddenly she sang along with the musicians, her clear soprano soaring above the buzz of the room . . . *"I will understand, always, always . . ."*

All of these things Susan Rose, writer and reporter, noticed. Then she stopped watching and was aware that Mike Browne could dance quite well when he chose. Perhaps he only chose when the music was so slow it wasn't really dancing at all. She was no longer a child with a stuffed toy, no longer a professional observer. She was a woman and a lean man's body was next to hers, pressing, making its presence felt, and she responded, like cellophane on fire. "I know you, bright girl," he said, "I know you from somewhere."

"That's what I've been thinking about you. Captain. Were you really a captain?"

"Would that make you like me better?"

"Of course."

"Yeah, I was a captain. If you have dinner with me tonight I'll tell you all my stories and later I'll take you home and show you my ribbons."

"Gosh, I can't. I have a date."

"Break it."

"I don't do that. It's not nice."

"Learn not to be nice. Nice people lose out on life. I have a date, too. It's a couple of phone calls."

After the last waltz they took the picture.

"Come on," someone said. "Before Kitty gets dressed let's have a picture of all the young people." The photographer had lined them up. Two rows of smiling faces, like figures in a shooting gallery.

In the front row, left to right: Jay Lawrence, Lily Welles, Red Jones, Kitty Jones, Gus Gladstone, Diana Weatherby, Peter Plainfield.

In the second row, left to right: Susan Rose, Mike Browne, Carol Plainfield, Dolly Gladstone, Willis Metcalf, Jack Weatherby, Mimi Bryan. (Absent: the baby sister, Natalie Jones, still throwing up in the powder room.)

"God, I think we're thirteen," said the groom, looking directly at Susan Rose, the presumed thirteenth.

"No, we're not," said Susan, who, unlike Red Jones, could count. "Fourteen. Twice seven. The luckiest number."

"Zat so," said the groom. "Well, whadya know."

"Susan always knows," said the bride, sticking her tongue out at the groom. She smiled her best smile. The flash went off. Then, weaving just slightly, she went upstairs to get dressed.

So it wasn't thirteen. The stars were right, according to Kitty, horoscope addict, who had had the whole occasion cast. And no one was wearing bad luck black. Indeed, everyone said it was *the* great wedding picture of all time, a classic of its kind. Members of the wedding proudly displayed the photo in silver and leather frames, on bedroom walls and baby grands, as a symbol of all that was good and happy in life. Still, if it had been thirteen, would that have given the future a shape? Would that have explained what followed, as one by one pictures were removed from frames, torn up and thrown in the trash, or burned, till finally one bleak day a woman who thought she was losing her mind began decorating hers with obscene graffiti?

But that fine day they were all smiling, all fourteen. That spring day was the beginning.

Chapter Four

The day turned into a soft evening and a brilliant night, and through the evening and the night and the next blazing yellow morning, Mike Browne and Susan Rose fell in love. "Love!" said Mike's cousin Tom, son of raucous old Uncle James, "She saw dollar signs, he saw a gorgeous pair. What's love got to do with it?" Well, what does love have to do with any case, when you think about it, Susan said. What *is* love? When she asked Mike, he answered, "You'll never know till you've lost it."

They started across Ninetieth Street and down Park, part of a laughing reeling group. Nobody quite knew what to do at that indeterminate hour; four thirty of a Saturday afternoon. It was too late to shop or go to the movies, too early for cocktails, too much wedding booze for a squash game. "Tea," Mimi Bryan suggested, "it's tea time!"

"Tea?" said Willis Metcalf. "What's that?"

"I'll see you all later," Gus Gladstone said, grabbing Dolly, turning in under an awning. "I'm going to sleep it off."

"*Sleep?*" said Willis Metcalf. "What's that? I know. Let's drop in on the Duke, he'd love to see us . . ."

One by one they moved off till just Mike and Susan were walking down Park, not knowing where they were going, but glad to be rid of the others.

Over to Fifth and into Central Park they walked, discovering that they were both fast paced; discovering, too, that they both felt the same way about the city spread around them, sapphire and rose and gold in the late afternoon light. They adored it, passionately, indiscriminately. Their very different points of origin met in this affection. New Yorkers to the core, they loved the noise and the smells, the flashing traffic and lofty buildings and crowds. They loved to tell off the tough kids who hustled and talk back to the traffic, swearing at the near-miss drivers. "Up yours," he'd yell . . . "Will you *watch* it," she'd scream. They loved the glaring concrete and the twinkling mica that danced on the pavements. They loved the steps of the Metropolitan Museum (and took a quick mocking run through the Browne wing, filled with furniture and paintings they both declared graveyard stuff) and the shrieking children on roller skates. They cherished the balloon man and the Cracker Jack vendor, the seals in the zoo, and the jagged mysterious skyline of Central Park West. They paid homage to the wild spray of the fountains in front of the Plaza and the waving flags, to Tiffany's and Bonwit's, Cartier's and St. Patty's and the big gilded jock of an Atlas in front of Rockefeller Center. ("My dentist is in there." "Mine, too.")

Walking along its grandest avenue, they proclaimed the springtime city the gayest, brightest, most thrilling in the world, city of the future, center of art and commerce and opportunity, hub of the nation. And they pitied anyone who had to live anywhere else.

They sat in a dim and cavernous hotel cocktail lounge, not drinking at first, not saying much, sobering up a bit, wondering perhaps what the hell they were doing, besides looking at each other and, accidentally, touching.

"A martini," he said presently to the waiter. "Very dry. You?"

"A ginger ale."

"Is that part of your religion?"

"That's the Mohammedans. I just try not to drink too much. Wine, champagne, at a wedding or with dinner, great. But in college and when I first went to work, I used to drink such a lot. My God, in my business sometimes it seems that's all you do. You've come back, Mike, to the land of the three martini lunch. And publishers' parties, office parties, art openings, meet for drinks, meet for dinner, meet after the theater. It's a life floating in scotch, gin, and vermouth. I'm attempting to dry out."

"Tell me something, bright girl," he said brusquely. "How old are you?"

"Why?"

"Just wondered." The look was shrewd, inquiring, a look that pushed nonsense aside.

"Old."

"Like how old?" he persisted. "I'm crazy about older women."

"Like old." She hesitated. But the lie wouldn't come. "Like twenty-eight." Almost twenty-nine. Almost thirty.

"My God, you are old. Gin is the only answer. Waiter, another martini."

"Gin kills me."

"Me too. So you have to keep me company. I like a girl to keep me company, every step of the way."

"O.K., it's your funeral."

"You don't look twenty-eight. You could lie."

"I often do. Don't you tell. Don't you give me away." She drew her breath, took the plunge. "How old are you, Mike?"

"Not very."

"Like how much not very?"

It was his turn to hesitate. "Like twenty-three."

"My *God,* how could you be that young? You don't look that young. How come you were a captain at twenty-three? You must have done something terrific . . . no kidding . . ." She talked furiously to cover embarrassment.

"Hey," he said taking her hand. "Hey, Miss Rose. Does it matter?" His eyes held hers. They were old and wise, a satyr's eyes buried in a boy's face.

"No. I'm crazy about younger men." She smiled. The sweet half-moon smile. *Go.*

"Cheers."

"Here's to you."

Taking a sip, she made a face, then took another sip. She never had liked the taste of gin, though she liked the effect. In his company she learned once more to drink the brew because he drank it.

"Tell me before I make a fool of myself," Mike Browne asked, "is there a guy? Am I wasting my time?"

A pause.

"No," she answered, because at the moment, instantly and forever more, there was no one except him.

Memory. Horrible memory. Cruel exact precise memory. Two people beginning. What else in the world can match it?

"I don't want another," she said. "I want dinner. I'm starved." None of the regular places seemed to suit her, those cunning *boîtes* in the East Fifties and Sixties where his world and hers sometimes met, the odorous ones with smudged purply menus and pretty tinkling names, Le Veau D'Or, Le Canari D'Or, La Petite Maison, Le Marmiton, L'Aiglon,

Charles a la Pomme Soufflé. None of the amusing atmospheric romantic places appealed, nor any of the hidden away joints he suggested, this one in Chinatown, that one in the Village. "I'm sick of the Village," she said, "sick of being hidden away. Everyone I know wants to hide me away. What is it about me?"

"God, you're difficult," he said finally, beginning to laugh. "All right, where do you want to go? The Colony?"

"That's not a bad idea. I think that's a great idea."

He laughed even louder. She liked his laugh. It was warm, and broke over her.

"What's the matter, aren't I dressy enough? Am I that wrong? Don't you have enough money, rich boy?"

"Oh, yes," he answered to all questions.

Later they would go to out-of-the-way places, hide from the world. That night in the white and gold gleam of the Colony, sanctuary of the rich and famous, with waiters hovering and people from other tables nodding and waving to Mike Browne and staring at Susan Rose, they courted as frankly and swiftly as those birds who dance, ruffle feathers, and leave in front of their intended mate a shiny pebble. So in conversation they danced before each other, telling light tales of their lives. So, ordering special dishes from the captain, discussing vintages with the wine steward, he ruffled his feathers. So when an acquaintance of hers, a best-selling author who could afford the luxury of dining thus, stopped at the table on his way out to speak to her, she ruffled *her* feathers, showed off a bit. And so when everyone had left the restaurant and the captain said with mock severity, "Monsieur Browne, is there anything else?" and they were still trying to decide whether or not to go to a midnight movie, he ceremoniously placed before her a shiny pebble drawn from his pocket. Only it wasn't a pebble, but a gold disk.

"Present for you," he said.

"What is it?"

There was a blurred face on it.

"It's an old Roman coin. Very rare."

She held it in her hand, felt its smoothness with her fingers.

"A dozen of these would make a lovely necklace," she said.

"I have a dozen," he said. And then, "You asked me this afternoon what I was going to do with myself, what I wanted. Twenty-four hours ago I didn't have a clue. Now I know. I want you. Can I have you?" He grinned, to make it a joke if she wanted to take it as a joke. But she wanted to take it very seriously.

She looked at him and saw how young he was, how spoiled. Sitting in this particular restaurant she thought all the things people later accused her of thinking about, of money and soft living and open doors and power. She saw a game she might win, felt her heart leap like a salmon.

"Maybe," she said.

"Hey, Mike, you know you left a hundred-dollar bill instead of a ten for the tip?"

"Did I? Oh, well, my grandfather made a hundred thousand dollars a day. I wouldn't know how to spend a hundred thousand dollars a day if I tried."

"I could think of some ways."

"You going to give me a nightcap?" he asked in her doorway, as she fished for her key, flashing his sweet wise guy grin.

"You know something, Michael Richards Browne?" she said, "You've got a real Mick smile. The first boy I ever went out with had a smile like yours. Name of Kelly. Good *night*, Mick."

"Not good night."

He took the key from her and kissed her, very gentle shy little kisses, like a sixteen-year-old who hasn't known a lot of girls, shaking his head, rubbing his nose against hers, and her heart pounded stupidly. She couldn't believe the way it pounded for such silly kisses. "I like you," he said. "I like you a lot." "I like you," she said. Then he really began kissing her, not gently at all, and she saw he was no novice, no sweet boy, but a veteran of many campaigns, an expert who was used to getting his way with women, who knew exactly what to do.

"Hey, Mick, take it easy," she said, with the greatest effort pushing him away. Instantly, just kissing, she wanted him, just as instantly, dancing, she'd wanted him. For a minute she couldn't remember why she had to send him away; why she shouldn't have him right away; suddenly she couldn't remember why she shouldn't do something idiotic, why she had given up gin. Then she remembered. "Really, good night." It seemed silly, but there was nonetheless a very specific and inflexible timing to these affairs, rules to be followed if she was going to play this game to win.

"Oh, to hell with all that," he said, reading her mind. "To hell with schedules."

Pause.

"O.K.," she said.

"The place is a mess," she warned him as they rode up in the rickety elevator that swayed like a reed bridge in the wind. "I left this morning in such a hurry."

"That figures. That's part of the picture."

"Are you tidy?"

"Very. When it matters."

"When's that?"

"On a boat. Camping. Mountain climbing. In the army. Fighting. Running a company."

"Oh," she said, not knowing much about these things that formed his life.

Actually, it was the mess, the books and papers and publishers galleys, the magazines and mail, the piles on every surface combined with high ceilings and pretty moldings and the fireplace that gave her living room distinction. The flat had once been the library and solarium of someone's elegant private house. It was a good deal—low rent, fair-sized living room, a closet for a kitchen, granted, but a big old-fashioned bath and a cheerful bedroom not much larger than the old fourposter bed she had fallen in love with one day in a thrift shop. Most of the other furniture was that of a resort hotel, blonde wood, blue coverings, Swedish modern bought at a Macy's sale, not a single souvenir of the apartment where she'd grown up because she couldn't stand the horsehair and mahogany of home. Besides the oversized bed, the only object with any personality was a scarred but honorable rolltop desk, at this moment unfortunately open to the mess of Susan Rose at work.

Mike went to this desk, as Susan made motions of picking up, pushing shoes under the sofa, thrusting old newspapers and dirty cups behind the kitchen arras. He played a few notes on the typewriter and picking up a page of manuscript, began reading aloud, mockingly, phrases she had thought pretty. Quickly and fiercely, she flew at him, pulling the paper away, slamming down the desk.

"Well," he said. "The lady has a temper."

"Don't fool around. It's not finished. That's my novel, and I'm having a horrible time with it. I may throw the whole thing out the window. It's my work, but I hate writing. If you want, I'll give you something I've had published. You won't like it, though. I know."

"It's proof you exist, that desk, isn't it? We all have something like that we don't want people to make fun of."

"Damn right. What's yours?"

"Anything. Whatever I'm doing at the moment," he said, arms around her, lips in her hair. Then, "That is a terrible dress. Is that how they taught you to dress on Riverside Drive?"

"Listen . . ."

"Don't you know you're not supposed to wear red to a wedding?"

One by one he undid the shiny buttons, till the dress dropped to the floor, a shed skin, the red petals of Susan Rose.

Chapter Five

"You all right?"

"Mmmm."

"Say something."

"Mmmm."

She was aware of a breeze coming up, a rattling door, the feel of a damp sheet at her back, his smile in the darkness.

"Can I turn on the light?"

"No."

"You're not the boss anymore. I want to look at you."

"Well, *hold* it, let me get the blinds."

Released, down tumbled the Japanese matchstick shades; as released, some moments earlier, down she had tumbled and lain still, inert.

"O.K.?"

Click.

Complete knowledge, perfect happiness. The moment. Having made love like that, to look at each other like that.

"I'm enjoying this movie, Susannah, better than the one we were going to see." Hands at work, lips and tongues and fingers at work once more.

"So am I."

"Have you ever seen one?"

"A *movie?*"

"A blue movie."

"What do you mean, seen one? You know about those USO girls. I've starred in one."

"Really? Not in the last one I saw. Ugly girl."

"I'm not ugly."

"Sure aren't. You're beautiful. My God, you're beautiful. Except for that. You didn't tell me about that." Lightly, with a finger he traced the bumpy violet scar smeared like finger paint down her stomach. "Somebody really hacked you up. What is it?"

"Appendix. I nearly died."

"I'm glad you didn't die. Funny, though. I thought you'd be perfect."

"I thought you'd be perfect. You didn't tell me about these," putting her lips to the two hideous tattoos, the tangle of arrows above his heart and the gravestone on his left forearm, wreathed in poison pink roses, the only flaws in an otherwise great body—smooth Ganymede from the waist up, bull from the waist down.

"I thought only navy boys had tattoos."

"I did it when I was in school. Big dare."

"But why?"

"Why else? To bug my mother. I love bugging my mother."

"Are you mean?"

"Sometimes."

"Will you be mean to me?"

"Probably."

"Then I'll be mean to you. I like things to be even. Eye for an eye, you know, tooth for a tooth . . ."

"Kiss for a kiss. Come here, Susannah, come here, you . . ."

"Hey, Susannah, where are you going?"

"To get some milk."

"Milk! Wouldn't you know. I guess you don't have a beer?"

"Sure I have a beer. What do you think I wash my hair in?"

"Look at me! I think we've started something."

"I think we've started something, too."

"I mean, really."

"I mean, really, too."

"Here's your beer. Watch out, you're going to spill it. Damn."

"You *are* so beautiful. So . . . slick. How many years can you keep a figure like this, Slick?"

"What a funny question, Mick. I don't know. Why?"

"Just wondered, Slick."

All lovers have nicknames, silly private bedroom names. Theirs were Mick and Slick.

"Who's that?" looking at the photograph by her bed, the only one in the apartment.

"My mother."

Don't make a crack, she thought, don't say the wrong thing, please, don't spoil things. But he only said, after a while, "She must have been lovely when she was younger. Is she here in New York?"

"She's dead."

"I'm sorry. Long ago?"

"The summer I graduated from college."

"How, Susannah?"

"Cancer. She lived long enough to see her scruffy little kid standing in a cap and gown, summa cum, Barnard College. She was a history teacher. I was her prize pupil."

"My old man died that way. It stinks. When I go, I want to go out like a light. And what about your father? Where's his picture?"

"I never knew him. He disappeared when I was four years old. He was some kind of failed musician. He played in movie theaters and in department stores demonstrating sheet music. One winter morning he took off for the West Coast to look for greener fields and never came back."

"No wonder you wanted to change your name. What happened to him?"

"My mother finally established that he died somewhere in California."

It was too much: a sudden grounding. She wondered what he would do to get them back up in the air. What he did was typical.

"That's rough," he said, with genuine feeling. "Really rough." Then grinned. "But the answer to a young man's prayer. An orphan."

It was awful, but she knew what he meant.

"Go to sleep, orphan," he said, for the last time switching off the light.

"I'll try. Good night, Mick." (First of how many good nights, how many thousands of nights, good and bad?)

In the recesses of what was left of the night, she heard him cry out, groan. He was trying to say something—a name—she couldn't make out; she reached over to him, held his shoulder. "What?" he mumbled, "what?" and then "O.K., O.K." and was quiet.

The smell of coffee woke her. Sun filtered in from every direction through the blinds. The bedroom had been the plant room of the private house; and she felt like a plant that had bloomed overnight, a big gorgeous begonia. She felt herself naked, was aware that she ached, remembered. Saw the place he had been, and was no longer.

"Mike," she called, "hey, Mike . . ."

Putting on a wrapper (surely stained and hopelessly wrinkled), she went into the living room where she found him dressed, drinking coffee, a stack of Sunday papers beside him, ready to face the world except he hadn't put on his jacket and his uncombed hair stuck up like a cockscomb. "Hello, darling," he said, standing up, smiling at her, and oh, what a great way to wake up, to be smiled at by Mike Browne and have him open his arms to you.

"Jesus, Susannah," he said a little later as they sat on the sofa together, "this is some establishment. One lemon, one quart of milk, one carton of moldy cottage cheese, one grapefruit, no butter, no eggs, no sugar, no marmalade, no bacon, no bread, no cream. You entertain a lot at breakfast?"

"Never." Yawning. Remembering something. "You had a bad dream last night."

"I do that sometimes."

"Want to talk about it?"

He shook his head. "God, you look sleepy," he said, touching lightly her cheeks, her eyes.

"And you're so *awake*. Are you always this awake in the morning? What time is it?"

"Late. Ten thirty, darling." She liked the sound of that "darling." A meaningless word in most men's mouths; in his a resonance, a gift. Something vaguely thrilling about the way he called her that.

"Ten thirty! That's dawn. It's Sunday. Let's go back to bed."

"Can't. Gotta get going."

"*Why?*"

"Because it's Sunday, darling, and at twelve thirty I have to be out on Long Island for lunch with the family."

"Oh. That's too bad."

The sun was gone, the day was gone; the monumental hangover arrived.

"I thought . . ."

"You thought what?"

"Nothing."

For five minutes she made bright conversation to cover disappointment, while he studied her. He seemed to be coming to some sort of decision.

"Did you want me to spend the day with you? Is that why you're being so phony all of a sudden?"

"No. Of course I didn't. I just didn't think you'd have to rush like this . . . *yes,* of course I wanted to spend the day with you. I *hate* comings and goings. Deadlines. Curfews. It's my fault. Women are so *stupid.*"

"Want to come with me?"

"You're not serious."

"Of course I am. You want to come? I'd love you to come. I don't want to leave you, either. It's just another one of those phone calls."

She decided that Mike Browne was no coward. Or was it simply that he enjoyed bugging his mother?

Chapter Six

She was a city rat. The country made her nervous, and the part of Long Island that they headed for that Sunday made her the most nervous of all. Just driving through it with Bill Wolfe on the way to Westhampton where they sometimes went for weekends (beach didn't count as country), she felt uneasy. Once in search of a restaurant they had explored a bit off the main highway. They had passed through Sands Point and Roslyn, Manhasset and Glen Cove, Locust Valley, Old Westbury, Old Brookville, Syosset, Oyster Bay. An impression had been fixed in her mind of ugly brick and stucco villages, 1910 Tudor. In each successive town she observed the same shabby railroad station and shiny garage, the same main street comprised of market, five-and-ten, movie theater, laundry, cleaner, liquor store, pharmacy, bar-and-grill, maybe three or four of each in the larger configurations with a funeral parlor, a high school, and two churches, one Episcopal, one Catholic. Whatever their populations, they seemed to Susan charmless toy towns no child would care to play with, servant towns for the surrounding estates.

Beyond stretched an impenetrable leafy countryside, presenting no vistas or open spaces, only threatening *allées* of trees, high walls, ten-foot iron fences and gates guarded by crenelated stone houses, miniatures of the castles and chateaus and palaces and manors hidden within. Now, knowing that before too long they would be stopping in front of one of those gates, honking for the gateman, she felt acutely uncomfortable, wondering what on earth had possessed her to come.

"Funny it should make you nervous," Mike said, as they drove along, top down, in the souped-up secondhand jalopy he had bought when he got home. "It's home to me."

He pointed out landmarks. Here he had bicycled. Through there he had ridden his horse. Here was the spot, eight miles from home, where he'd been captured after running away from a battle-ax governess. There, that dirt side road, was lovers' lane, where he'd parked and necked and had his first girl. Here he had started on a race with the state police, the goal Southampton, Mike Browne the winner.

"Home is where the heart is, right?" she said. As a massive iron gate opened and closed behind them, Mike Browne waved to the gatekeeper, shouted a greeting. The man shouted something back, and they both laughed, a ritual of sorts.

"Not where the heart is," he said. "Home is where you once thought you were terrific."

The gravel road rose steeply and wound through woods for several minutes. She could imagine a boy hurtling down that road on scooter, sled, or bike, and later, last summer before the war, in his first car. She could imagine, too, a boy exploring those woods, in those tangled green depths, escaping from the nursery strait jacket, counterfeiting wilderness and adventures. Then the road came out of the woods, into air, light, lawn, straightening itself, cutting across green velvet grass to a straight wide brick house painted white with sky-blue shutters; a hilltop house that seemed to float on the grass. On that grass she saw ghosts, ladies in ballooning dresses and cartwheel hats, men in blazers and white flannels and straw boaters. "This is the kind of house Gatsby couldn't get into," she said.

"Who's he?" said Mike Browne, the self-proclaimed illiterate.

"A character I know," she said.

"Name-dropper."

But when she later made the same remark to his mother who had been placing the house and its view in the context of Long Island geography, Violet Browne said, "That's interesting, you know. Mr. Fitzgerald came here once. He was brought by people we knew, and he said something almost like that."

Susan and her mother-in-law got on, right from that first day. Violet did what she could to stop the marriage, for all the obvious reasons plus a few special ones of her own. But once she saw she had lost, she lost gracefully, so gracefully Susan couldn't stay angry. Like Gloria St. John, Violet Browne was full of charm. "My dear, I liked *you* the day I met you," she'd say, "but I thought it would be complicated. Too difficult. I thought you were each in your way too much for the other. I believed my son would be better off with a younger girl brought up as he had been, of the same background, the same religion. I didn't realize he was so strong, so *original,* my son, nor you such a . . . quick study." Violet had a talent for making obnoxious remarks in such a reasonable way that Susan would find herself almost agreeing.

Entering her house, Cherryhill, was terrifying and Susan wanted to bolt to where she belonged. She had been in other large houses in the course of her work for the magazine, but the people she interviewed were, mostly, as new to the houses as she was: self-made people of vigor and talent with brand-new money to spend, new power to exert. This place smelled of old money, old power, held on to for generations. From the walls of the great central hall stared family portraits by Gilbert Stuart and John Singer Sargent and Boldini. Up the wide curving stairs had walked robber barons, Edwardian beauties. Down the banisters, escaped from the top floor, had slid groomed little children in lace and velvet knickers. The big rooms off the central hall, filled with important furniture and great vases of flowers, had contained kings and presidents, senators and sportsmen, the heads of banks and railroads and steel companies and great Wall Street houses, and other companions suitable to the Brownes who were themselves in all those things, railroads, steel, banks, Wall Street and who had holdings in half the states of the union. "Platinum people," Susan had called such families once in a story, "rich, discreet, boring, and indestructible." Through the French doors leading to the terrace she could hear their voices now, the silvery chiming of the women, the booming of the men punctuated with loud, assured laughter.

"Hey, darling," Mike said, as the maid took her coat and the butler their orders for drinks, "they won't bite. I'm crazy about you, darling," he said. He always would pick the damnedest times to say things. "I woke up this morning and looked at you and decided I was absolutely crazy about you. So you'd better get used to this place. Come on."

"What makes you think I want you to be crazy about me?"

"We're out here," a voice called.

Brilliant sun flooded a mossy brick terrace crowded with people and ironwork furniture, a place treacherous as quicksand for an outsider. Susan was glad she had done what he suggested, worn a sweater and skirt instead of a silk print. A breeze was blowing, cooling the bright air. It was always cool on this hill, she could tell, even on the hottest summer day.

And everyone was in country clothes except for Mike, still in yesterday's blue suit, and one ancient lady who was dressed, as if for a garden party, in flamingo pink silk (her skirt almost to the ground, revealing heavy ankles, nurse's shoes) and an enormous pink hat, a confection of straw, veiling, tulle roses. It was from the side of this rosy apparition that a woman in soft gray tweed with gray hair detached herself and came toward the latecomers. The face of the woman was not soft. Her skin was weathered, her features knife sharp, her eyes an intense blue: the mother, unmistakably, of the son.

"Darling," she said to him, "always the last, but never mind, time for one drink."

"My mother, Susannah Rose," he said.

Susan didn't contradict him. She allowed him right then to take over her name, her person, put her future in his hands.

"So glad you could come, Miss Rose," said Violet Browne. "Michael Dick never gives anyone much notice or I would have telephoned you. Michael Dick, go talk to Aunty Grace, she's been pestering about you, and for God's sake tell her you love her hat." A trace of the South in the voice (she was a King from Virginia, direct descendant of a signer), a whisper of magnolia, wisteria; steel in the eyes; surprising warmth in the smile. "I'll take Miss Rose around."

"Susannah."

"Of course. Susannah. Now move, Michael Dick." And Susannah saw the formidable lady in pink melt at the approach of Mike Browne, saw him kiss the pink aunt on both cheeks, French fashion. "Oh, my dear, dear boy," she said. "God, Aunty Grace," he said, touching the brim of her hat, "where'd you get it, did you grow it?"

They were almost all Brownes. The clan, Violet said, and how nice to have someone break it up. There were his Uncle Eustis and his Aunt Laura, his Uncle James and his Aunt Betsy, his cousin Tom, his great-aunt Grace King, his older sister Priscilla, known as Puss, and Puss's husband, George Chase, and

Puss's best friend, a face from the day before, Diana Weatherby, whose husband Jack was playing in a golf tournament. Frizzy-haired, freckled, with pointed nose and bright little eyes, Puss in no way resembled her brother; she looked like a pretty fox. Di Weatherby, however, *was* a fox gone wild disguised in puritan dress. (The day before she'd been in a gray silk print; today it was gray flannel with crisp white touches.) As for Mike's brother-in-law, he resembled a well-groomed bulldog, all of which seemed fitting when you learned that the girls had gone to Foxcroft and George to Yale.

"Well, Brownie," said Di in the husky insinuating voice that was her trademark. "You must really like that suit. You must *sleep* in that suit. You'd better break down and get yourself some clothes."

"Is this an occasion?" Susan Rose asked Mike's mother. "A birthday?"

"No," said Violet, "I like to gather when there isn't any occasion. You could say today is a celebration of the blooming of my trees. It's been so cold they're very late this year."

They were incredible, those trees that gave the house its name: gnarled, round-shouldered, with branches dripping pink and white blossoms, a great crescent of them behind the circular terrace. Beyond the long length of lawn more trees—dogwoods coming on, cream and then scarlet rhododendrons and banks of tulips and forget-me-nots. "It's fantastic," Susan said. "Really breathtaking. I've never seen anything like it. Except in a book with pictures of English gardens . . ."

"It's a garden," said pink-cheeked, pipe-smoking, aggressively tweedy cousin Tom, put off by the excessive reaction.

"Susannah is quite right, Tom," said Violet Browne. "It *is* fantastic. Even Jimmy says it's fantastic this year. You and my son have no eyes, no feeling whatsoever for growing things. I remember Mike when he was little . . ."

She made it easy at first, talking continually as she showed

Susan around, making small jokes about her son, telling stories on him, commenting on the day, the view, the foliage. Then, sitting the stranger beside her on the terrace ledge, she began the process known as "placing," which was not quite so easy.

"You aren't related to the Baltimore Roses, are you?"

"No. I'm from New York."

The voice puzzled Violet, you could see that. Susan spoke in her softest, breathiest accent, the one she had copied from certain women on the magazine, the one she reserved for special interviews, special people, but through the pastel wash broke the cement hardness of her real accent, rock-bound, fighting New York alley cat.

"Or those Hudson River Roses?"

"No."

"But you do know the story about the Hudson River Roses . . ." It was the first of many such stories Susan Rose was to hear. Jew stared wide-eyed at gentile.

"My Rose is made up, an abbreviation of something else," Susan was saying polite but angry, when Mike joined them. Behave, his eyes ordered, *behave*. "When I sold my first story someone convinced me that Susan Rose was a good pen name."

"Well, that's fascinating," Violet said, pursuing it no more. "Tell me, what do you write?"

"Short stories. Articles. Captions. I'm also an editor. I get other people to write things for me." She produced her credentials.

"Of course," Violet said brightly, "you're Kitty St. John's friend from the magazine. Yes, now it all . . . imagine my idiot son bringing home a brilliant girl. Yes, I *have* heard about you. Ah, I see Hadley . . ." The butler was at the door. "Lunch everybody, come on. We'll talk more later. I'm *fascinated*," she said again. "Really, Michael Dick, you might have given me a clue. Now tell me about my old friend, Elena Worden," Violet said as they walked into the house. Susan told her. "Well," Violet said, "well, my dear, I must say your frankness is refreshing."

From the dining room you could see more enchanted trees, more tender green lawn, and beyond, rolling pastureland flanked by woods, and a spot of blue water: the scorned Long Island Sound. Susan thought it the prettiest, most peaceful view she had ever seen. She knew then that beach days with Bill Wolfe and the Westhampton gang were over forever. She liked the solid excellence of the room, with its blue gray walls, its foaming seascapes and stately oils of sailing ships (the Brownes were great sailors). She liked the furniture, so highly polished she could see herself in it, and the intricately patterned Oriental rug at her feet. She marveled at the solid excellence of the lunch, imagined decades of such Sunday lunches: clear soup with a float of whipped cream; rare roast beef; puffy Yorkshire pudding; roasted potatoes, crisp as chips; vegetables bright and fresh as the grass outside; and a great pyramid of a dessert, combining sherbet, ice cream, cakes, and meringues—a dessert so splendid that when it was brought out the more boisterous members of the table clapped. (Later, when in many such houses she choked on gray beef and stringy vegetables, she would realize that the rich mostly serve abominable food and would appreciate even more the style of Violet Browne and learn from it.)

Even the conversation was something to be enjoyed, once she caught the rhythm. Placed between Mike and his Uncle James, she fell immediately into easy talk with that old boy, who had manners and a twinkle, and who was inclined to treat a stranger kindly. While Mike, at the head of the table—the father's place—talked to the aunt on his right, Jimmy Browne and Susan Rose happily found a subject, suggested by the giant silver marlin hung above the fireplace: fish. James Browne, it turned out, was a famous, record-breaking fisherman whose catches adorned walls of countless Browne houses, and the marine life halls of natural history museums all over the country. Susan, no sportswoman, could nonetheless recall the most joyous moments of her childhood as those on vacation with her Uncle Dan, in a smelly boat off the coast of Miami, fishing for tuna, barracuda, and marlin. She had words at her command and could summon up sea, weather, smells, triumphs, misfortunes, so Jimmy Browne said, over and over, "Yes, yes, my dear, you've got it, that's it, that's *it.*" She amused him. From fish they moved on to other matters of the sporting life, and for the space of that lunch Susan Rose was the greatest outdoor girl in the world, a veritable Diana, when in truth she was a lazy orchid, an overblown Aphrodite.

"I can talk to you," Jimmy Browne said, as many men would say to her. "Can't talk to most women but can talk to you."

She basked in the old boy's admiration, in the enjoyment of making a conquest, preening herself a bit, all the while aware that Mike, apparently in intent conversation with his aunt, was continually looking sideways at her. His looks mixed approval with surprise.

Toward the end of the meal Jimmy said to Mike, "You must bring this charmin' young lady to see us. We've been havin' the best time. Want her to see some of the things we've been talkin' about. You goin' to be around, boy?"

"Awhile."

"What are your plans?"

Shrug. Con man grin. "I'm going up to Camp Browne for awhile. Then to California. Dave Brocker's putting his head in the noose. Remember Dave? I gotta stand up for him. Then, who knows. Probably south. Eddie Bernardos wants me to do the back country in Chiappas with him. How about joining us?"

"I'm grounded. The old ticker's been actin' up," said Jimmy Browne, former member of The Explorer's Club, boss of Camp Browne. "Maybe when you get all that out of your system you'll come see me downtown. We could use some young blood."

"I'm not cut out to be a businessman."

"You shoot crap, don't you?"

"I have that reputation."

"This postwar market is going to be the greatest floating crap game that ever was, bigger than the twenties. I think of it as the last frontier."

"Could be." A shrug. "Anyhow," turning in Susan's direction, "I expect we'll have time to come visit you, Uncle Jim. Don't you think so, Susannah?"

"Oh, I think so," she said. Something passed between them, some secret thought transference that by no means escaped the keen eye of Jimmy Browne.

Afterward the women went to the terrace. The men remained in the dining room for cigars and jokes, and for a few minutes Susan sat with the fox faces, Puss and Di. But they talked in a language she didn't understand, about people she didn't know, though Di Weatherby, slightly less provincial than the other, made an attempt to include the stranger in the conversation. "This person we're talking about," she'd say, "this place . . . this party . . . I have to explain . . . this *character* has a reputation for being just a trifle intemperate, *n'est ce pas?*" looking at her friend, raising her eyebrows, "a teeny bit *in*judicious in his choice of female companionship . . ." and they'd burst into giggles, and Susan still wouldn't know who they were discussing, why they were laughing. Then, again Violet Browne came to rescue her and took her into the rose garden, and the cutting garden, and the kitchen and herb gardens, and explained where they were in relation to the city, to Long Island Sound, the ocean and surrounding towns. They had their conversation about Scott Fitzgerald and about books that sprang to mind. "We are readers, you and I," Violet said. "There are going to be less and less of us, I fear. My daughter doesn't read at all. My son reads only for information. Well, you know my son." She hesitated. She smiled. She had something else to say. "Perhaps you'll have an influence on him. You seem a very directed girl. He is somewhat without direction at the moment, which is not unusual among these boys just home, but with him it seems to go deeper."

She was easy, confiding, almost cozy that day. But then she knew her son or thought she did. She knew his father, knew about wild oats and wrong girls, about bugging mother. Her son liked to surprise her, and she liked to surprise her son. "I've enjoyed talking to Susannah so much," she said, walking them to the car. "I hope you bring her again."

"Well, darling, I'd say you made a big hit with everyone," he said, as if bestowing an honor on her.

"Well, darling," she replied, as they curved and swerved back through the woods, "I'd say your mother took the wind out of your sails." She was partly teasing but suddenly and unaccountably angry, now that it was done, now that she'd gone through the wickets, passed a few tests.

"How's that?"

"You were playing a little game, weren't you, taking me out here today?"

"She enjoys a good fight. No one enjoys a fight better than my mother. But then again, sometimes she likes to turn the other cheek."

"Is that a crack?"

"No. Just an observation. Speaking of cracks, what do you mean, I was playing a little game?"

"Bringing a girl you picked up at a wedding and slept with to mother's Sunday lunch. That's the kind of thing that appeals to you."

"Sure it does. Doesn't it appeal to you?"

His bright blue eyes held hers, his impish grin forced a return smile from her.

"Doesn't it?" He was offering her a gift—a better gift than

love—the knowledge that life is indeed a game, but not a little one—a great one—and he would teach her how to play.

"Yes."

"Then don't get edgy with me, *you,*" he said, pulling up to the gate. "I've slept with a lot of girls, but I don't bring them home to Sunday lunch. Damn," honking the horn. "Where is that joker? Take the wheel a minute while I get the gate. And watch the brake."

"I don't drive. What do I do?"

"Don't drive? You *are* a gutter snipe. Get the gate then."

It was big and heavy with three intricately tangled golden initials at the center of each side and golden finials on the vertical bars: a work of art, Mike told her later, that had taken eight burly Italian workmen to hang.

She stood aside as he drove through, then got back in.

"I'll have to teach you to drive," he said. "You ski?"

"No."

"Play tennis?"

"No."

"Ever climbed a mountain?"

"No," beginning to laugh.

"Ever shot rapids?"

"*No.*"

"I'll have to teach you all those things, beach bum. You are a beach bum, aren't you?"

"You've *got* it! And what will I teach you?"

He frowned. It hadn't occurred to him that she might teach him something.

"To be kind," he said, after a long pause.

Chapter Seven

He drove with one hand, while the other caressed her.

She noticed his hands. They were not especially beautiful. You would have expected other hands to go with that face and body, narrow elegant hands with long fingers. These were square, stubby, powerful, and on the little finger of the hand that moved possessively over her glittered a ring. A big, heavy, gold ring with a diamond in the middle, not the sort of jewelry you'd expect this sort of boy to wear. It was a gambler's ring, a gangster ring, flashy and vulgar.

"Can I see?" she asked, taking his hand off her. "Can I see your ring?"

"I never take it off," he said, replacing his hand. The stone glittered.

"It's unusual. Not the sort of thing I'd think you'd wear,"

she teased, again taking his hand, forcing it to rest innocently in hers. "A gangster ring."

"It belonged to my grandfather. The one who made a hundred thousand dollars a day. He *was* a gangster. Michael Richards. I was named after him. It's my good luck. Don't you have something like that?"

"Long ago. A watch. The only thing of my father's I ever had. I lost it. After that I swore I'd never cling to anything."

"I lost this ring once. I knew if I didn't find it I'd die. Fortunately—unfortunately, some might say—I found it."

It was a long story involving a summer resort, a car, a beach, a girl; it took the rest of the way into town to tell. Car keys and ring misplaced through carelessness, lost in the sand. A hunt at twilight, in the growing dark. The sort of story she was coming to recognize as particularly his, funny at first, then twisting into something less funny, something cruel. He had become unreasonably angry, blaming the girl, and to appease his anger he had made her do certain things.

"What things?"

"Never mind what things. Things."

And as she was doing whatever it was he made her do, submitting to whatever it was he was subjecting her to, by accident the keys and ring were found. "But she never spoke to me again. Found the ring, lost the girl. What do you make of that?" Grinning, the grin gone crooked.

"Strange," she said, lighting a cigarette, freeing herself from him. "Like a story I once wrote about myself and someone. I swore . . ."

"Swore what?"

"Never mind."

"Swore never to take up with a boy like that again. Right? I'm not like that anymore."

"See. The girls I like have always been forbidden," he said, stretched out beside her smoking a cigarette. She lay peaceful and quelled, the jagged edges of her smoothed. That was what he did to her, she thought, took all the odd sharp pieces of her, the cutting edges, and made them into something round, soft, and smooth. She tried to explain to him, but it wasn't the sort of thing he followed. Besides, he had something he wanted to say, whether she wanted to hear it or not, something she had, unfortunately, no trouble following whatsoever.

"I mean forbidden. *Out. Verboten.* In the summer I always liked a town girl, like the one I told you about, never the ones I was supposed to like. First girl I ever really fell in love with was a nurse who took care of my old man when he was dying. No old bats to see *him* through his final agony. 'A chip off the old block,' he told me, when he caught me making out with Miss Giovanni when we thought he was sleeping. Then there was a dancer, my fifth form year in school. She thought I was a senior in college. The school thought she was the dentist. And a waitress in a *trattorìa* in Rome."

"Listen, Mick, what the hell are you trying to say?" She was beginning to separate again into jagged pieces.

"I'm trying to say that after years of messing around with one girl after another, there you were, a guest at my friend's wedding, all those other girls wrapped into one, but not forbidden. A classy dame. A friend of the bride's. It was like some goddamn miracle."

"Hey, Mick?"

"Yes, Slick?"

"I couldn't be more forbidden, or more wrong. And you know it."

"I know it. And I love it. You going to be my girl?"

"I guess so."

"No one else's."

"No."

"I'm very jealous."

"So am I."

He had explored her body. Now, in the dark, gently, sleepily, like a blind man, he explored the features of her face, memorizing them in his fingers.

"Did you have your teeth filed? They're so even."

"That's from chewing things like pencils, paper clips, and rubber bands. I used to be very nervous."

"Still are. Except after you've been screwed. I guess the cure is to keep screwing you. Do you know your nose turns down?"

"What do you mean?"

"The point goes down, like it had a tear at the end of it."

"That must be the wailing wall in me."

"I mean, Di Weatherby, Puss's friend, has a nose like yours, but the tip doesn't go down."

"Fuck Di Weatherby."

"No thanks. Hey! What sort of talk is that from a lady?"

"I'm not a lady," proceeding further to talk to him in a way no lady ever would, not even in bed, a way that drove him wild.

That night he didn't cry out. Just kept waking her or she him.

"I'm afraid you're not getting much sleep," she said. "Go to sleep."

"I have years to sleep."

"Years for this, too."

"You think it lasts like this?"

"If I thought it didn't I'd shoot myself."

"Me, too."

"Everything's so corny."

"Like?"

"Like I feel I've never been with anyone else."

"Have you been with a lot of people, Susannah? I can't tell about you. You're tricky."

"Not a lot. No one. That's what I mean. You make me feel like a damn virgin."

"You make me feel like myself."

The next morning it was she who left him sleeping, he who found her dressed, ready to go, sitting on the sofa with the papers, drinking coffee.

"What the hell," he said sitting beside her.

"It's Monday morning."

"Be sick."

"Can't do that. Don't *want* to do that. Today is going to be fun."

"You look sharp. I didn't know you could look like that. You always look that sharp to go to work?"

"Sometimes. When something special is happening. See, today I'm having lunch at '21' with . . ." she named the famous movie star in town to promote his latest film.

"The hell you are. No girl of mine is going to have lunch with that guy. I'm coming along."

"Don't be childish. This is business. I'm doing a story on him. One of my perfect bitchy little interviews. Or maybe not so bitchy. I hear no girl can resist him."

"O.K. Rosalind Russell, beat it. Give me a farewell kiss."

In the dark burnished glow of the bar at "21" she talked to the famous movie star. At the next table sat Mike Browne. Alone. Out of his blue suit at last, suavely, sportily dressed in light gray flannels, bright tie, conspicuous in his looks, pretending not to recognize her. Cool as could be, eating an elaborate lunch, drinking a fine bottle of burgundy, talking to the waiter and the wine steward, shouting a greeting to someone standing at the bar, being joined, for a moment, by a man Susan recognized as Tony George, the columnist, looking airily around, occasionally dropping a look on her. Halfway through lunch she broke up.

"What's going on?" asked the famous star, a handsome, grizzled, aging boy.

She told him. Until then their conversation had been a disappointment. There is an art to the interview, not mere questions and answers, but the setting up of a relationship. A good interview, for her anyhow, was a *coup de foudre*—a highly personal experience, instant love, instant dislike, instant something, from which derived her style, her originality, her writing personality. That day, under the eye of Mike Browne, the experience was instant nothing. She couldn't operate, couldn't get through, couldn't generate the magnetic field, couldn't concentrate. Finally, partly furious, partly amused, utterly self-conscious, she explained to her companion. He understood, because he understood about lovers, was a well-known and inventive one himself. He found her confusion appealing.

"Ask the boy to come over," the star said, thinking the whole thing a good joke, beginning to enjoy himself and to discover that Susan Rose was after all, as the press agent had promised, an experience.

There followed a historic lunch, a hilarious three-way conversation during the course of which the professional Susan Rose vanished, pencil ditched. She simply lived that lunch and witnessed what she would witness again and again: Mike Browne connecting with someone. He wasn't anything, really, except rich, and handsome enough to go on the stage, but some quality about him made people treat him as if he were something more. As he and the flashy actor traded service stories, she saw that he had the kind of rough personal charm that cuts across lines, class, geography. She recognized a seducer of humans. So with some trifling stories and a few caustic remarks he made the great man laugh, and made her laugh so hard she got the hiccups. He finished off the afternoon by taking them on a tour of Abercrombies, his favorite shop, where the star was recognized, and they parted in a small crowd of fans, with a shouted agreement to meet much later at El Morocco's. All in all, it was the beginning of a turbulent three-way friendship and the inauguration of Susannah and Mike, public couple, item (duly noted the next day in Tony George's *Town Talk*). Years later the same star said to a reporter, "Yes, I knew them at the beginning. It was a beautiful thing to see, two people falling in love so hard, so publicly."

Chapter Eight

At Del Pezzo's, the lusty old Italian restaurant, favorite of violinists and tenors and the *Time-Life* crowd, for the fiftieth time in eight months Susan had lunch with Bill Wolfe, who was still under the impression she was his colleague and sometime property. Under the eye of the jolly, avuncular waiter who always tended them, anesthetized by a martini and half a bottle of Soave Bolla, she performed the operation.

"Bill?"

"Mmmmm? Sorry, mouth full. This is good today. You aren't eating a thing. And since when the gin?"

"I'm not hungry. Want some of mine?"

"Sure. You know I always want some of yours. Have I told you lately what a pretty girl you are?"

"Listen, Bill!"

"Yes, dear heart, I'm listening. Don't you feel well? Oh, I get it. It's that time of the month. That's why the gin."

"Bill, I can't see you anymore."

"I know. I *said,* it's that time of the month. It comes with the moon. You're feeling guilty again. Don't. You're in the clear. You've been absolutely fair. You've told me you don't love me. When I want to move on, I will. Believe me. Meantime . . ."

"Bill!"

"You're *not* ruining my life, kid."

"Bill, damn it, you make it hard. See, I've met someone."

"As of when? A week ago you sure as hell hadn't met someone. A week ago was pretty nice, Susan. No?"

"A week ago was a week ago."

"What did you do, you bitch? Get drunk and go to bed with some guy you met at that fancy wedding?"

"Don't talk like that. This is different."

"We were all different, Susan. All the guys you've been through. So tell me about this one. Does he have a name?"

"Mike Browne."

"*Mike Browne.* That sure is a big jump up from Bill Wolfe. Jesus. I interviewed some Browne last fall, the one who collects all the impressionists."

"His Uncle Eustis."

"His Uncle Eustis? Is that right? You've met the family already!"

"As a matter of fact, I have."

"You haven't wasted any time. But then, as I remember you didn't waste much time with me, either. My dear mother and my dear aunt in Forest Hills often mention you, ask why I don't bring you out anymore, recalling those *gemütlich* days, just a few months ago, when you watched mother in the kitchen and sat around talking to auntie, listening to her stories about the good old days in Vienna. And who was it you ditched for me? Oh yes, that photographer. I know his brother.

His brother still talks about you a lot. I guess Bill Wolfe, the war correspondent, was a step up from him, and he was a step up from the army lieutenant and the lieutenant a step up from the corporal. But who's going to be a step up from Mike Brown? Those people own half of New York."

"Stop it. You don't understand one thing about me. I like him. Really *like* him."

"Brother! Give me my violin."

"You *are* a violin. And badly out of tune. I liked him from the first minute I laid eyes on him. I didn't know who the hell he was. Just liked the look of him. It's never happened to me like this before. Now I know it's the only way."

"You're full of crap, Susan. And you have a *very* short memory. He'll never marry you."

"Who's talking about marriage?"

"What else? Let's face it . . ."

"We've just met. He's just out of the army. It's idiotic. He's *younger* than I am. There are a lot of problems."

"Still, that must be what you have in mind, because you're a smart girl, but I tell you he'll never do it. I know his type. I knew some of them in college, from a distance, thank God. Porcellian Club boys, Fly Club boys. Porks and fleas. Every now and then a rich pork or a rich flea will marry a showgirl or a movie star, or a singer, or even a gorgeous cigarette girl. Someone who makes people's heads turn when she walks into a room. But Susan Rose, a bright, glib, Jew girl on the make, with a gift for words, and a certain talent in the sack? Forget it."

"I make people's heads turn."

"Minor league, baby. You are very minor league as a head turner."

"You watch. I'm going to make people's heads spin around like tops. To *him* I am a gorgeous showgirl."

"Just last week you told me you wanted to make people's

heads turn with what you wrote, make people laugh and shiver and cry with words."

"That was last week."

"I wish you luck."

"I'll bet."

"Truly I do. I'll write the 'Milestone' myself. Or maybe we can get an item in 'People.' I'd trim up a little, though, if you want to hold on to him. Once the first bloom is over. You may be a little careless for a boy like that. A little hairy. Keep your nails clean and your legs shaved, that's my advice."

Chapter Nine

"Come on, lazy bones," Mike said, one hot Saturday morning. Summer was beginning to put its paws on the smooth spring air. "Come on, Miss Rose, get your clothes on." Already dressed, he was standing over her as she lay drowsily in bed wondering what he was up to now.

For five weeks they had fought and loved and chased each other and invaded each other's territory. He sometimes referred to himself as Mick, and she had abandoned Susan for Susannah entirely. Her office would never be the same after him. His club, the Knickerbocker, where he was officially staying, though he had more or less moved in with her, would never be the same after her. They had been on a great spree and the whole town was talking about them. When they walked into a restaurant or night club people stared and whispered (and Brownes everywhere had fits). On her behalf he had knocked a man out, a drunk who said the wrong thing. To amuse her he had brought a horse to a cocktail party, a monkey to church. He had kept night clubs open till dawn. He had arrived at a friend's house with a jazz band at midnight. Just to give a party he had rented the penthouse apartment where later they would live.

On his behalf she had done nothing so conspicuous. She, a girl who needed a lot of sleep, had simply given up sleeping.

But this morning the pace had caught up with her. "Why go anywhere?" she asked, yawning, feeling the laziness that sets in with summer; also feeling pressured, since he had said that in another two weeks he'd be gone, and what would she have as a souvenir? A few beautiful art books, an embroidered sweater, a Venetian glass ashtray, a string of antique coins mounted in heavy gold? But no engagement ring, no simple ten-carat solitaire to prove she was his, to hold the option, so to speak, for his return.

"Mick," she held out her arms to him. "Do you know I adore you? Do you know that? You make me so happy."

"What's your problem?" he said. "What makes you so nice this morning. Come on, up!" Flicking water at her from a glass beside the bed. "I thought we'd get married today. I thought we'd drive to Elkton, Maryland, and get married."

"*Married?*" The prize, the jackpot, the gold ring, so easily achieved, without all the desperate games and tricks she'd planned, a proposal simply thrown at her, as he was now throwing her some clothes, a pair of pants, a bra, a cotton sun dress, a pair of sandals, her wedding raiment.

"Yeah, why not? Everyone's doing it this year. Wouldn't you like that, Susannah? To marry me? Wouldn't you like me to make an honest woman of you?"

"I am an honest woman."

"You know what I mean."

"No." It had become their chant . . . You know what I

mean . . . No . . . That's the way life is . . . Is not . . . That's human nature . . . Doesn't have to be . . . Accept things as they are . . . Never . . . "But yes, I'd like to marry you, I'd like that very much," and turned on her side, too moved for a minute to look at him, afraid if he saw the awful nakedness, the needfulness of her, he'd take the offer back, because he didn't like her weak or needful.

"Only," she said, when she could speak clearly and steadily, "only," she said, pulling on a wrapper instead of going into the bathroom with the proffered clothes, "I don't want to go to Elkton, Maryland. I don't want to do it like that."

"No?" He sat down beside her on the bed, put his arm around her. "What did you have in mind?"

"I want to be married properly."

"And how would that be? You want to give yourself a wedding, orphan, give yourself away?" Smiling, teasing.

"I have someone to give me away. I have my uncle in Miami."

"You want to be married in Miami?"

"No, stupid. I just mean I have someone to hand me over to you. I want to be married at Cherryhill. In your mother's garden."

A pause. A withdrawal of arm, smile, teasing tone of voice.

"You have to be joking."

"I'm not joking."

"I don't think you quite get the picture of my mother, Susannah. She's being a bitch." Up and down the living room he paced while she made coffee, clattering some. "You know when I was away last week and you got so mad? I spent that day in her august presence in Southampton, where she's staying with Uncle Eusty, summoned no less, so she could tell me some things. I wouldn't repeat them to you. Let's just say she does *not* approve of you and me."

"That's to be expected. I'm sure you can charm your mother into doing anything you want."

"I'm not interested in charming bitchy women. I'd run half-way around the world to get away from one."

"What can she do? Can she do anything about your money?"

"Hell, no. She can't *do* anything. But she can hurt. She can make me feel guilty. I don't like feeling guilty and I don't like to be turned down. I'd rather not ask in the first place, rather not promote an occasion in which I will yell at my mother and be made to feel like an ungrateful shit."

Twenty-three wasn't very old, she suddenly saw. Twenty-three, even with those years in the army, was a baby. What was she doing with this baby?

"Don't ask her. Tell her. Say mother or mummy or mater or ma or governor lady, or whatever the hell you call her, I'm going to marry Susannah. Since Susannah has no home, I'd like to be married quietly in my home. You're the man, remember? You sit at the head of her table, Mick."

"I wish you'd stop calling me that. Look here, she's my mother. Since you don't have a mother, which as I've often said is one of your major attractions, lay off."

"O.K., wise guy. I'll lay off. Here's your coffee."

"Come on, darling," he said more gently, "don't spoil things. Let's go. And then, what's done is done, and believe me she is great about the accomplished fact. She'll sell you to the whole world."

"Gee! Wonderful!"

"You know what I . . ."

"Damn you, I'm beginning to. I'm beginning to know exactly what you mean. I don't think I want to marry you. But if I did, if I was that crazy, I'd want to do it right. Eloping is a fake. When I get married I want everything to be kosher."

"What's that mean, Susannah?"

"*Kosher*. You know. Like hot dogs. On the level. Good. Approved. By the way, I've decided I don't want to be called Susannah. My name's Susan. Susan Rose."

"Well, baby, there hasn't been much attention paid to what's kosher so far," putting down his coffee cup, looking at his hands, his feet. "I wouldn't think that a girl who takes what she wants the way you do, without any qualms, would suddenly talk about what's good and right and approved and . . . *kosher.*"

He went on a bit more. She went on a bit more.

She told him how she felt about marriage. She told him how she felt about herself. He saw she expected to be taken seriously in a way he was incapable of taking her. He saw she wanted to be esteemed in a way he was incapable of esteeming her, of esteeming anyone different from himself. He saw she would not be categorized and it was necessary for him, as it was for all boys like him, to put people in categories. He saw she considered herself his equal.

"Gus Gladstone," he said, as if he were quoting God instead of one of his drinking companions, "thinks I'm out of my mind. He says mixed marriages never work and he should know. He's funny. He said, 'you know what you'll have to do to join the tribe'—and at your age it'll really hurt."

"You know what I'd like to do to Gus Gladstone."

"You can't. He's my best friend."

Angry and confused, Mike began quoting to her more of the things that were being said, by his mother, his uncles, his friends, things concerning her race, her appearance, her origins, her age, her speaking voice, her manner of dress; things concerning their unborn children, concerning her behavior and morals, as if their own daughters and sisters and girl friends and wives were not in and out of more beds and less honest about it.

And presently she told him to get out. Leave.

Abruptly he stood up, knocking over the rickety coffee table that she had never remembered to fix.

"This is where I came in," she said.

"This is where I go out. I thought you were some other girl

when I picked you up at that wedding. I'm glad I found out before I made a serious mistake."

Only long after the door had slammed and she'd watched him walk angrily down the street and disappear around the corner, did she begin cursing, did she throw the necklace he had given her against the wall, and, for the first time in her life, poured herself a drink at ten in the morning. Then she called her friend, Kate Bellow, the *Life* photographer, and arranged to leave town within an hour. She could move fast when she had to. She caught the early afternoon ferry for Fire Island; and stayed up late at night, drinking with Kate and Kate's lover and other former companions, talking about things a world away from Mike Browne. She knocked herself out with sun and waves. And for the first time, she skipped work for three days, playing sick, keeping her hand off the telephone, gambling on the fact that Mike Browne would frantically be trying to find her.

Chapter Ten

Deeply tanned, flushed, slightly frantic herself, she walked into her living room and found him lying on the sofa, reading an old news magazine, beside him an empty glass and a jar of peanuts. On a table stood an enormous vase of American Beauty roses, four dozen at least. She glanced at the card: "To Susan Rose from Mick Browne, you never know till you've lost it."

"Lost what," she said, "your lunch?"

"What took you so long?" ignoring the remark, tossing a peanut in the air, catching it in his mouth. "You're out of tonic. Gin and ginger ale is a vile drink. You left the ice trays out. The bed's not made." He, too, must have been in the sun somewhere. He was tanned, a study in brown and black, insufferably handsome, and she wanted him horribly.

"You are a bastard," she said softly.

"I know," he said, also softly. "You like that. If it was any other way you'd be bored." The smile came out, broadened into a perfect Mick grin. His arms opened. She didn't go into them. Just stood, looking down at him solemnly.

"I suppose you want me to say I'm sorry," he said.

"Something like that."

"When I was a kid that was the worst, being made to apologize."

"You're not a kid anymore."

"You think?" Long, struggling silence. Then: "Will you forgive me for those rotten things I said?"

Further silence.

"Yes," she said.

Then he stood up and took her into his arms and her give-away heart hammered wildly, and she was almost ready to bend her will to his, do whatever he wanted, anything to have him, keep him. But fortunately he did not guess that, not then.

"You win, Susan," he said. He kissed her. "I wonder," he added, "will you always win?"

"You can call me Susannah."

Lovers, duelists, antagonists, blind humans, locked in mortal combat. Whatever they were and were to become, they assumed their roles that day.

A week later they were married, just as she wanted, in the garden at Cherryhill. In attendance were only the immediate family—his mother, his sister and brother-in-law, his great-aunt Grace, her Uncle Dan, up from Florida for the occasion —and Kitty and Red Jones, the witnesses, and Dolly and Gus Gladstone, because nobody did anything in that group without Gussie's blessing and send-off. Performing the ceremony was a judge, though naturally no ordinary justice of the peace, but a distinguished member of the state supreme court who years later would say, "Yes, I married them. I have no other comment on the affair. No comment."

The capitulation of Mike Browne to Susan Rose seemed complete, but he would never tell her what had made him change his mind, nor how he had forced his mother to agree to the Cherryhill ceremony, the judge, to any of it. "Blackmail," he said. "An ordinary case of blackmail. Or bribery." However much she teased, he wouldn't say more. "You'd just get mad. You got your way. I have to have a few secrets."

So, displaying an equivalent tact, or embarrassment perhaps, she did not describe to him her hassle, two nights before the wedding, with her Uncle Dan. Generous, vigorous, brusque of temper, wiry of hair, gum chewing, cigar smoking Dan Rubinstein looked a little like Groucho Marx, a little like Michelangelo's *Moses*, and behaved that night as Moses might, if Groucho were playing him. Mike, Susannah, and Dan had had dinner in the dining room of Dan's hotel. Susannah did most of the talking and the two men addressed each other entirely through her, both of them immediately at their very worst, Dan all Yiddish Art Theater, Mike all Groton-Harvard. Upon Mike's departure, Dan began shouting at Susannah as he had shouted at her all her life. He had paced up and down the hotel bedroom while Susannah sat on one of the beds, shoes off, cross-legged, furiously smoking, her ritual posture for argument with Dan.

He had told her what he thought of pups like Mike Browne, of rich goys, of goys in general. He had assured her such a boy, for all his money and flossy connections and good war record, was no match for a brilliant girl like herself, who could go anywhere, be anyone, the new Edna Ferber, the new Dorothy Thompson, the new Dorothy Parker. He told her she should be ashamed of herself, marrying a kid practically half her age and insisted she reconsider this ridiculous wartime match, as if the war weren't over.

"Your Aunt Rachel and your mother would turn over in their

graves, God rest their souls," he said, squeezing out a few tears.

"I don't think so," she said. "Your late wife and my dear mother were at once very romantic and very practical, which about sums up the situation."

"You're going to be bored, old darling, I know you. So bored," he kept saying.

"I wouldn't think *you* would think money boring," she kept saying.

"It's as if you were marrying a Martian. You have no language, no possible language in common with such a boy."

"Listen, Dan, we have a language all right."

"I know that language. That language is quickly learned and quickly forgotten, Susannah" (he, too, had never called her anything else).

"Bums," he shouted finally. "A buncha bums," dismissing Mike Browne, his kind, his world. He was turning around, said Dan, going home on the first train in the morning, would not have any part of this wedding, and meant it. He was that sort of man. So Susannah had to apply her own bit of blackmail, break his spirit slightly, in order to lead him, tamed, to the sacrifice.

At the wedding, old ham that he was, as sneaky a charm boy as the great Mike Browne himself, Dan Rubinstein behaved with perfect grace, perfect dignity and good humor, and when Mike said, "I've decided I like the old phony," Susannah simply replied that it took one to know one.

Her dress was the color of thick cream and brand new. Her underclothes were absurdly old. Her mantilla was borrowed from Kitty Jones, and for blue there was the magnificent star sapphire newly glowing on the fourth finger of her left hand, and the matching bracelet that had been Violet's wedding present. Like sapphires were Violet's eyes that afternoon, fixed on her new daughter-in-law with a curious expression, not of liking but of a certain grudging respect. Mike's own eyes were virtually closed, his hangover on his wedding day monumental, wages of one last binge with the boys who hadn't been invited to the ceremony.

Of "the Squad," only Red and Kitty Jones, Gus and Dolly Gladstone were present. Red and Kitty, both of them sunburned, peeling and rather subdued, just returned from their Bermuda honeymoon, seemed unable to grasp the occasion. Kitty smiled a lot, but she didn't seem quite thrilled with her friend's runaway good fortune. ("I was *jealous,*" she said later, "of the way you two were.") Dolly, sparkling, winking in the sun, was furious at Gus who was on crutches, one leg in a cast up to the groin, an arm in a sling, aftermath of a speedboat accident in which by all rights he should have been killed. "That was his seventh life," Dolly said. "I've kept count. Two more to go. Then . . ." finger across the throat. "I won't weep." "You'll look good as a widow," Gus said. "Black's your best color."

For a moment or so, even on her own wedding day, Susannah observed the by-play and was amused. She breathed in the summer smells, the new mowed grass, the roses and the privet, as well as her own perfume, which she had applied too lavishly, as usual. She listened, in the instant before the judge began to speak, to the shriek of birds, the buzz of insects, and saw a bumblebee in the vicinity of the groom's nose and thought, "Later I'll get hell for this," having been the one to beg for an outdoor ceremony.

Then the gravity and the purity of the moment overwhelmed her. There was no Mike, no Susannah: for one second she had a sense of something larger than either of them as they listened to the judge's words, then turned and looked at each other in perfect seriousness, a pair of lovers formalized, frozen into two figures called a bride and groom, a husband and wife. *Till death do us part . . .*

What a relief, though, when it was all over, when they had drunk their last glass of champagne, given their parting toast, relished their final triumph, as they drove off: the sight of Dan Rubinstein deep in conversation with Miss Grace King. What a relief when they had cleared the ultimate hurdle—the reporters from the tabloids waiting outside the gate with cameras and questions (she waved; he gunned angrily right through)—and, driving to the Sherry-Netherland where they spent the night before leaving for the Adirondacks, they could laugh and mock the whole occasion. Then, always trying to educate him, she repeated Eugene O'Neill's version of the wedding promise, written into the playwright's own first marriage service: "Love, honor and obey till love do us part."

"We might beat that rap, smart girl," Mike said. "Just might." And meant what he said.

Chapter Eleven

The honeymoon, neither of them quite knew why, was not a total success. The honeymoon might have given them both pause. They should have taken that honeymoon out and examined it together, instead of instantly burying it deep down in the ground of their separate selves. That honeymoon was a warning to both of them.

She hated instantly what he loved. Camp Browne itself, she acknowledged, was an object to be appreciated. She enjoyed all that rustic luxury, the deep beds and Indian blankets and fur rugs, the built-in furniture, the cool air and the smell of pine wafting through big windows, the healthy food, the evening fire, the boathouse, Lake Browne sparkling through tall evergreens, the satiny swims, the canoeing and trout fishing, the Indian trails through deep woods. For about five days she enjoyed it, though she could have done without the sleeping porch and the sunrise reveille of birds. Then she began getting nervous, whereas he, restless elsewhere, was peaceful as a lamb, happy as if he were home, as if Cherryhill were no more than a way station.

"Sometimes I think I could live here half the year," he said one day, rowing her around the lake.

"Dear God, doing what?"

"Working on the place, cutting trails, fishing, skiing in the winter, studying the rocks and the birds, gassing with people in the village. Imagine having your very own mountain and lake and forest. These are the greatest Christmas trees in the world, did you know that? This is a working Christmas tree farm. Wouldn't you like to run a tree farm?"

"I'd cut my throat. No offense."

Another day, sitting on the big front veranda: "It would be a wonderful place for you to write," he said.

"I've given up writing. I've junked that awful novel. That's finished. I don't like writing any more."

"Oh."

"You sound disappointed."

"I thought you were good at it. I thought if you wrote something a simple guy like me could understand instead of all that quivering, fancy stuff, you could write a great book."

"Thank you, but I've given it up. Writing for me has always been a means to an end. You're my end. The life we're going to have is my end. Write? What for?"

"Oh."

"Oh, what?"

"Oh, nothing. I had a picture of you, up here, writing, that was all."

She was very jumpy, in any case, the former Susan Rose, trapped in the Adirondacks, wanting to do something, wanting to see a movie, shop, poke around. But once you'd poked around Brownesville for an hour you'd done your poking, unless you liked sitting around chewing the fat with the locals, which Mike enjoyed but she didn't. So he announced for his and her pleasure a week's camping trip, including a climb to the summit of Mt. Marcy. "I thought you could *drive* to the top," she said.

Better to have stayed put loafing around Camp Browne. When he said climb he meant climb. Every symptom she'd suffered her one summer at camp, courtesy of her Uncle Dan, came back: blisters, bug bites, rashes, insomnia, night fears, vertigo, aching back, aching legs, inability to catch her breath, terror of the woods, of snakes and birds and toads and all wild creatures, terror of looking over a ledge, of slipping, of breaking her neck. Whereas he, nimble as a goat, whose wartime ribbons were won for mountain warfare, knew no fear, never got tired, never got blisters, sang (who never sang at any other time) as she panted, and treated wild creatures as if he were some sort of American St. Francis. She called him a sadist. He called her spineless. Both wondered aloud who it was they'd wed and why.

"How am I ever going to turn you into an outdoor girl?" he was cooking in front of the tent the trout he'd caught and cleaned.

"I don't think you are."

"You need to work up your nerve, Slick."

"I have nerve: It's called 'some nerve.' There! I've made you laugh. First time in days."

"I want you to be happy. I want to make you happy."

"I will be. You do. It's just this mountain and these woods. Wait till we get to California. I love California. I'll be nice there. Wasn't I nice in New York?"

"Moderately. I want you to be nice all the time."

Last night of honeymoon, full moon shining on two naked bodies tangled in an Indian blanket, on a sleeping porch.

He: "Beautiful. So beautiful, my wife. The most beautiful wife any man ever bought himself. But needs loosening up. Maybe I should make you pregnant. Maybe that's what you want. To have a baby right away. I wouldn't mind."

She: "Good God, no! I've been working all my life. I want to enjoy myself for a while."

He: "Wouldn't you enjoy yourself having a baby? Usually girls like you, built the way you are, want kids right away. Six of them."

She: "Two. Two is the perfect family. One boy, one girl. But first I want to live a little. Don't you?"

He: "Oh, sure. I'm just curious, that's all. What the kid would look like. That's all. Forget it."

When you come right down to it, honeymoons are the devil's invention, for people who can't be alone together.

On the other hand, what followed those first weeks, as far as she was concerned, was an idyll, plain and simple, a careless, reckless, glorious kaleidoscope time, a gypsy time, a wander year with all the money in the world to pick up the tab. "This is more like it," she said, over and over. No sooner were they back in New York than they took off for the West Coast for a wedding in San Francisco, a fortnight of partying in Beverly Hills. Then they headed south. Mexico and Yucatán, to look at ruins, for him to do the rugged back country with a friend while she sat in Mexico City having her portrait painted by a world-famous artist. Then Guatemala, to visit a friend who owned half the country. Panama, Peru, Equador, Bolivia, Brazil, Argentina . . . he seemed to have friends, connections everywhere: South American boys he'd known at school, ex-service buddies, business associates of his uncles, friends working in oil and shipping concerns, friends investing, buying up land because these were the years when young men of a certain world were pursuing their fortunes south of the border, the great postwar frontier. Everywhere they went his enthusiasm waxed over one project or another, and they'd say, "let's never go back," but presently, of course, they moved on to the next place.

Finally, after nearly a year's wandering, surprise: he announced one day they were going home, that he was going to work in the family firm.

"Good," she said, "that's what I'd decided. A year's fun and then settle down in New York."

"*You'd* decided," he said. "You had nothing to do with this. I made a promise."

"Oh," she said, "so that was the blackmail. That was the bribe." Smart old Violet, no flies on her. Susannah could see she and her mother-in-law were going to get on very well.

But not before they had had the greatest time anyone ever had did they come home and settle down. He seemed to grow up. She seemed to have found a youth she'd never had. They scrapped, of course. Each was subject to swift rages should the other appear interested, even for an evening, in someone else. But that was natural, people thought, between such hot-blooded newlyweds, who seemed at times more Latin than the Latins.

All that can be said about such an unreal start in life is that when it was over the year seemed to have dissolved like a spoonful of sugar and counted, curiously, for nothing. At its end, Susannah and Mike returned to a sequence of wild welcome home parties, moved into the penthouse, and were pretty much as they had been at the beginning. Their marriage was still for all intents and purposes a love affair. She was happy to keep it that way for a while. No babies. No responsibilities. Just themselves in the silken aerie twenty floors above Central Park that certain catty women called "Cherrymountain" because, consciously or unconsciously, in style the apartment was so patently an imitation of Cherryhill, of Violet's style, a miniature 1920's country house set in the city sky.

Only in passing did Susannah note the disasters that befell, during the space of their year away, two members, like Mike and herself, of the Jones's wedding—the deaths of Lily Welles and Willis Metcalf.

Four months after Kitty's wedding, on a glorious night when Mike and Susannah Browne happened to be sitting in a West Coast café appreciating the beauty of gulls silhouetted against a torn red sky, back in New York, Lily Welles, the shining-haired playgirl of the tight dresses and loose reputation, died in agony of peritonitis following a botched abortion.

It was highly publicized at the time, involving as it did a glamorous and well-born girl, a fancy Fifth Avenue doctor and a ranking member of "the Squad," a titled Italian tennis pro, who for years had been cruising New York dance floors and Long Island beaches, delighting the men with his skill on the courts, the women with his bedroom eyes and bedside manner. Lily's father, Amory Welles, conservative Roslyn patrician, had forfeited the ancient right of a rich man to keep his daughter's name, in life or death, out of the papers. He prosecuted the doctor, who went briefly to jail, and gave the story to the press as a warning. So Lily Welles became in her untimely death unique: a symbol of the flaming youth of this second postwar joy ride.

Then ten months later, the following June, on another gorgeous night when Mike and Susannah were high in the Andes in a town close to the stars, Willis Metcalf, Red Jones's ebullient cousin, who looked like a horse, had climbed, while very drunk, the big oak in the Southampton garden of Jack and Diana Weatherby, had roared like King Kong to his friends assembled below, who were laughing, cheering the court jester on, and had swung out. Only he picked the wrong branch and fell, not very far, but in such a way as to hit the base of his neck on the side of an Italian renaissance lavabo, brought out from Diana's grandfather's place in Old Westbury when they'd torn the Old Heap, as Willis called it, down. For eight months, in Southampton Hospital, poor Willis lay dying, not even an animal, but a vegetable. Then mercifully he drew his last breath, enabling his family finally to give him the big New York funeral at St. James he deserved. And most mawkishly and luridly, in the pages of *The American Weekly,* Tony George, who had been there the night of Willis's fall, recorded his end. "Playboy Willy Metcalf" had, after all, been a favorite character among Tony's readers who enjoyed nothing more, next to a good murder among the very rich, than a gruesome death by accident.

Both these tragedies were noted briefly by Susannah, the former writer, now a society lady, at the huge housewarming she and Mike gave to open their apartment and celebrate the decorating, which had taken six months and, so the rumor went, half a million dollars. She observed, a bit flippantly some thought, that in fiction literary taste would keep you from such corny stuff as the ends of Lily Welles and Willis Metcalf, but that life had no literary taste. None whatsoever.

Then she put these deaths aside, because although they were all members of the same wedding, Lily and Willis had nothing, after all, absolutely nothing to do with her.

Part II

Chapter Twelve

With the death of Gus Gladstone in the fall of 1949, each and every one of the Squad might well have begun to wonder: who next?

In any case, this melancholy event had a lot to do with Mike and Susannah Browne. From the moment the news came, in the middle of a boisterous Sunday lunch at "Cherrymountain," Gussie's death spelled trouble.

This lunch was the sort of gathering, after three and a half years of marriage, Mike and Susannah had become noted for: amusing, overturning accepted practice. Sunday, after all, was the day most people of their sort went to the country; but soon after they'd moved into the penthouse, with its 360° view and spectacular midday light, Susannah had said: "Sunday is the day for the country to come to us." She had lured Violet and the uncles into town, inviting at the same time some young theatrical friends and made the mixture of postwar Broadway and prewar society work beautifully. Sunday pot luck Chez Browne became one of the more enjoyable occasions of New York life in the late forties, should you be lucky enough to be asked. This particular day seemed no exception. There was a convivial mix of Brownes for class, and celebrities for dash, of his Wall Street friends (Mike Browne, to everyone's amazement, in a few years had become one of the boldest, smartest young speculators in the postwar market) and her museum friends (Mrs. Mike Browne, to everyone's equal amazement, and over many dead bodies, had recently been elected, in spite of being Jewish, a woman, and excessively outspoken, to the board of the city's snobbiest museum). Also there, for old times' sake, were select members of the Squad, including the ubiquitous and powerful Tony George, Mr. Manhattan. (However you felt about the man, you asked him, and again, and again, because to appear in his column was part of your reality. If you hadn't read it in George, it hadn't happened.)

Appropriately, Tony got the news about Gus.

Lunch was in full noisy swing when a maid whispered to the columnist he was wanted on the phone. Twenty-odd people were crowded around one long table, the effect that of an informal Provençal feast, with wine, bread, and fruit on the table and in place of roast beef and Yorkshire pudding, an exquisite dish from the Midi, chicken and prawns. Everyone was laughing, arguing, gossiping, interrupting, shouting across the table, as was customary when lunching at the Brownes. The most exuberant conversations, it so happened, concerned the Gladstones; the upcoming divorce of Gus who a few weeks earlier, in one final and public scene, had ousted sassy Dolly. She was in Sun Valley preparing to sign a divorce agreement that was not, Susannah said, the most generous. He was in Maryland for a hunting weekend.

Tony returned looking grim but barely able to contain his

excitement. "Gus Gladstone has been killed," he said to Susannah. "The paper just called. It came over the wire."

Hurriedly, because he had to go immediately, the columnist told her what he knew which was by no means the whole story: Gus had taken off alone the previous morning in a Land-Rover to do a little grouse shooting, promising his hosts to be home for lunch. Instead, he had met some unidentified friends at a roadhouse, had gone from roadside bar to road-side bar, somewhere along the way picking up a woman. He had then apparently ridden off onto some back road where he had crashed. The girl had been thrown free, Gussie killed.

"Oh, *no*," people around them began to say loudly. Down the table conversations stopped. By the time Susannah reached her husband to tell him the terrible news, he had already heard.

"It's awful, Mike," she said, "just horrible," and should have stopped right there. But instead, out it popped, on the heels of a genuinely expressed sentiment, a typical Susannah crack. "But what incredible timing!" she added. "Instead of grass widow, it will be real widow's weeds for Dolly. Do you suppose she planned the whole thing?"

Over the next three days, in daily by-line articles, Tony George spun out the odd story of Gus Gladstone's last escapade. There was the identity of the drinking companions: one a Miami gambler, the other a former bootlegger. (Were they just drinking companions?) There was the character of the woman, a divorcee barfly in her thirties. There was, strangest of all, the fact that Gussie had not been killed by the impact of the crash but shot through the head, his rifle apparently discharged inadvertently. At the end of three days the case was closed, the death pronounced an accident. But had it truly been accidental? Had he known his drinking companions previously? Had he known the woman before? Was this a case of a rich boy thinking gangsters and thugs cute and getting in over his head? And what was behind it? No one could write a more breathless, speculative prose, barely skirting libel, than old Tony George, when he put his mind to it, and he had a field day with this one.

The night before Gussie's funeral, sitting in bed, catching up with a pile of newspapers, Susannah read every word and said to Mike, as she had said several times already, "It's fascinating. Awful and absolutely *fascinating*. And spooky. Remember Dolly the day of our wedding, talking about Gussie's lives?"

"That's a man dead," Mike said grimly. "What are you talking about, *fascinating*?"

She elaborated, doing Tony George one better. She might have given up her career, but she couldn't get away from stories. "If I were still a writer . . ." she said.

"You're not," he said. "*He was my best friend.* And all you've been talking about is how *interesting* it is. You should be married to Tony George. You two would make a great team."

"O.K.," she said. "I'm sorry he's dead because nobody should be dead and you loved him, but I didn't. I enjoyed dancing with him and going to the races with him and playing cards with him and receiving beautiful flowers from him, but I did not like him. He was a snob, he treated women like dirt, and he was an anti-everything, including Semite."

"A lot of people like that are. That's the way they were brought up. To be anti-everything."

"Are you?"

"No. I'm peculiar. They put braces on my teeth, but even my teeth wouldn't behave. However, after nearly four years of marriage to *you* . . ."

They could make a fight of anything these days and still make it up, as indeed they made this one up, somewhere in the recesses of the night, in the obvious way. But still the next morning they started out for Gus Gladstone's funeral with bad hangovers.

Now a funeral might seem an odd setting for such a shameless husband heist as occurred that day, except to anyone wise to the ways of love and the rich, such as Susannah.

In a church pew, behind veils and hymnals and tear-laden lashes, eyes can swivel, glances lock. In a vestry room or on a flight of stone steps, old friends will see each other anew; lovers reconcile, fall back in love; enemies embrace. In a dim bar or crowded living room, at a post-funeral collation, people who have sworn off each other forever will suddenly switch on. There is something about the tears and the jokes that causes the polite walls between people to fall. More to the point, there's something about the way a woman can look in black, frail, needful, more feminine than she ever has in her life; a man in a dark suit and a somber tie can suddenly appear vulnerable, guard down, open to attack. And, having known each other all their lives, a woman in mourning and a man in a pallbearer's suit can look at each other's puffy lids and raw noses and become strangers, and fall in love.

So, anyhow, it was with Diana Weatherby and Mike Browne the day they buried Gus Gladstone. "I know you," he and Susannah had said to each other the day they met. "I don't know you," he and Di Weatherby said to each other that morning. "What's *your* name? Who are *you?*"

Susannah first noticed Diana (and literally didn't know who she was) in the church, at the awful moment when the organ sounded the recessional and the cortege began slowly moving up the aisle. During most of the service she had been observing, as usual, taking mental notes of people, odd pairings, suppressed dramas (in particular the drama of Dolly, dulled, heavily veiled, sitting with her mother-in-law, rejected Dolly flown in from Sun Valley to mourn her soldier boy love and duly collect her lawful inheritance). Now even hard-boiled Susannah felt a *frisson* of awe, seeing all those pale, solemn, beautiful young men walking beside the flower-draped coffin of their friend, the most solemn, palest, and most beautiful of all being her husband. At that moment she knew what was *in* that casket. She thought of Mike in it, herself in it, Violet (two rows down to the right) in it, Kitty (sitting beside her) in it, every last one of them in it (she couldn't think of her mother, because her mother had been cremated, but thought of her mother's urn, sitting in the garden of her Uncle Dan's Florida house under the birdbath). Then something touched her and she felt sorrow and the most unimaginable tenderness toward her husband as he passed by. She wanted to repeal a bad forty-eight hours, wanted to catch his eye and tell him so.

But his eye could not be caught at that moment. What she did catch, though, one spotlight crossing another on a darkened stage, was someone else also trying, unsuccessfully, to catch the eye of Mike Browne. Across the aisle, one or two rows back, was a woman in black, maddeningly familiar but totally unrecognizable behind a brimmed hat and veil, who seemed to be concentrating on Mike, following him with her hidden eyes, turning over her shoulder to follow him till he passed out of sight.

"Who's that?" Susannah whispered to Kitty Jones as they stood up to leave. The woman in the black hat, now observed to be tall and wearing a Persian lamb coat, was moving purposefully, a little ahead of them, looking neither to the right nor the left, as if she wanted to speak to no one, smile at no one, but get out fast.

"You need glasses, friend," Kitty hissed. "That's Di. You only see her every week."

"I wouldn't have known her. She looks *awful*."

But Mike didn't seem to know how awful she looked. Coming out of the church after some minutes of hushed exchanges with various people in the vestibule, Susannah saw them standing together, a bit apart from a familiar group that had gathered at the bottom of the steps, Carol and Peter Plainfield, the Joneses, Kitty's cousin Jay Lawrence, Mimi Bryan and

Mimi's new beau, John Packard, the attractive young lawyer everyone hoped she would marry, and, as always, Tony George. Mike was looking at Diana as if she were something wondrous, magically appealing. Diana was looking at Mike as if he were her last friend in a world gone mad, something precious to be held onto. Indeed, she was doing just that, clutching his sleeve with a big freckled hand.

They seemed, the two of them, totally oblivious to everything around them: oblivious to the whispering people moving past them down the steps and getting into limousines, some of the people making little gestures of greeting that were ignored.

"Hello, Diana," said Susannah, who would not be ignored. "It's some lousy day."

"Shitty," Diana said huskily. Unlike Susannah, Diana didn't ordinarily use barracks language, only her own school-girl euphemisms. "So *shifty,*" or "so *gritty,*" she'd say, and "oh spit," or "oh shoot," or "oh schizo," or "oh Balzac," but today repeated, "So *shitty*. Why don't we go break a few windows."

"Take it easy," said Mike, looking at his old acquaintance as if he'd never seen her before in his life, looking tenderly at Diana Weatherby, with her red nose and stringy red hair and hideous hat, as if she were Daphne Parr, the new town siren, or Tootie Blake, the young actress.

"Should we go?" said Susannah to her husband.

"Why him?" Diana continued. "Why Gussie? When there are so many boring people in the world still walking around."

"*Mike* . . ." Susannah's voice was becoming imperious.

He looked startled as if for a moment he didn't know Susannah, either. Only a few hours ago, he had certainly known her as she had sat in her mirrored dressing room with the sprigged carpet and baskets of plants (exact replica, almost, of Violet's dressing room at Cherryhill). As she sponged on her make-up, brushed her hair, and contemplated her dark handsomeness he had come up behind her, and a dozen reflected Mikes had said, "Who are you today? Ava Gardner or Scarlett O'Hara?"

"Anna Karenina," she'd said.

"I'll tell you who you are," he said, beginning to smile, a pale moon sun of a smile trying to break through the overcast of last night's quarrel. "You're Susannah. Not like any actress or character in a book, just yourself, and if a person has seen you once, God help him, he'll always know you." That's what he'd said early that morning. Now, at noon, he didn't seem to know her at all, seemed to find the rich sabled sight of her out of key next to Diana and her black-framed plainness.

"Let's go," Susannah said. "It's freezing."

"We thought the Westbury. That's quiet." He motioned in the direction of the people gathered at the bottom of the church steps who were stamping feet, knocking knuckles, making sounds of impatience.

It struck Susannh, who in the end was always accurate, that in spite of the red nose and stringy hair, there was something singularly appealing about Diana Weatherby that day, her face bare of make-up, dusted only with freckles, her brown eyes magnified by welling tears. Her smile was brave when it came through those tears. Blessed with all manner of physical bounties, Susannah suddenly hated Diana for possessing the one attribute she lacked: a great, generous, open, all-American smile.

"I thought you and *I* were having lunch," Susannah said to her husband, talking right through Diana, not caring if she was rude.

A frown: don't be so thick. A nod in Diana's direction: can't you see she needs looking after?

"I don't want . . ." Diana began, sweet as could be.

"You're not," said Mike abruptly, and turning his back on his wife moved Diana off the steps, down the street. Susannah followed with the rest of the group and told herself he was being kind—a boy scout.

Chapter Thirteen

In the dark rose-colored Polo Bar Mike and Diana sat together at the far end of a series of tables, opposite each other, as if lunching *à deux*. Susannah was between Jay Lawrence, the village drunk, and Tony George, the village snake. Both men began talking at once, very loudly in post-funeral unease, unlike the two at the far end who were very quiet. Susannah ordered a double martini on the rocks.

"Where's Jack Weatherby?" she asked Jay presently. "You'd think he'd have shown up for Gussie."

"Montego Bay, I believe." Jack was currently "into things" in the Caribbean: resort development, gambling casinos, things like that. "Haven't you heard? Di's tossed old Jack out."

"I thought she adored Jack."

"How long can you *adore* anyone?" Jay drawled. His voice

was as thinned and transparent as his skin, which now looked like very old ivory, though he was scarcely thirty. Drink . . . too many women . . . boys . . . who knew what the trouble was. He was the odd one of the bunch and sometimes Susannah chose the role of being friendly to the odd one. "If you're the sort compelled to adore," he added. "You may *adore* pheasant, but if you had to have pheasant every day, after a while you'd get tired of pheasant, no?"

"No!"

"Well, we all know about you. *Fidèle.* Fido. You behave the way she seems to be," he inclined his head in the direction of Diana Weatherby. "But she really *is* the way you seem." Diana had taken off her hat, letting dirty, stringy red hair swing forward as she leaned across the table to Mike. He pushed a lock behind her ear as if he were dealing in silk. "What about *him,* though?" Jay said. "Were I you, sweets, I'd lock him in with a kid or two, you know?"

"Were I you, sweets . . ." Tired, suddenly, of being friendly, Susannah said something really quite offensive.

"Poor Diana," Tony George said. He, too, must have been observing them from time to time. "She's broken up about Gus."

"Did she love him?"

"Of course she loved him. They were all young together, long before you and I came on the scene. Di's the sort of girl Gus Gladstone was meant to marry, don't you know? Mike, too." He was a snake, though he looked more like a giant caterpillar today, fuzzy brown hair, fuzzy brown mustache, fuzzy brown suit. Death on women, some said, but not on Susannah. "Then it's not so amusing to have your husband go off with a nineteen-year-old blonde." (Women were said to find his clipped, Eton accent adorable; Susannah thought it came out of a can.)

"I thought she'd left him."

"No, *no*. She may have thrown him out. But for a reason. You *know*. Young ripe blonde. The Paxton girl."

"That makes more sense."

"I don't know. Your husband hasn't taken his eyes off her." A red-lipped smile forming under the mustache. "I hear he's to be congratulated."

"For what?"

"The Smassen deal."

"Oh, yes? I don't know about that. Way over my head." Never tell George anything, even if it's been printed everywhere: a Mike Browne order.

"I never would have thought Mike Browne would have settled down so. I wouldn't think it now, to look at him. I'd watch that, darling."

"What?"

"That. Those foxy horsy ones are like flypaper."

"You've such a warped view, Tony. All life is your column."

"Your warp, darling, is you can never see anyone else's woof. Lemme tell you something about flat-chested girls."

"Never mind."

"What they lack above they make up for below. It's a proved scientific fact that girls with small chests have huge . . ."

"Shut up, Tony."

"You know different?" The eyes were creeping up and down her now, as if to pry out her secrets. "I was trying to amuse you. You are very difficult to amuse some days."

"You revolt me," she said flatly. (A month or so later, when George wrote the first item concerning Mike Browne and Diana Weatherby and Susannah phoned him in a fury, he said, "Come, *darling*, I'm trying to amuse you, it's our joke.")

So, as happened to her in certain moods, Susannah Browne ended up talking to no one, sat smoking a cigarette, dropping ashes in untouched food, drinking the last of her double martini, observing the pose of Mike and Diana, who continued to talk in a tense, isolated way to each other. Presently people began to leave and she heard Mike's voice above the barroom drone: "Listen, idiot, it's your life," and Diana's: "Anyhow, you can still give me a lift downtown."

It was perfectly logical. Diana's divorce lawyer had offices on Wall Street. Mike, who always took the subway, was indulging sorrowing Diana who had probably never been in a subway in her life. Susannah couldn't have said why such a disagreeable picture flashed through her mind as she stood on Madison Avenue watching their cab take off with a lurch into suddenly dense afternoon traffic: a picture of two sad and slightly drunken people thrown against each other, two old acquaintances come into each other's arms by accident, staying there, and kissing each other, by no accident at all.

That night, with six people waiting, he arrived home an hour late, full of excuses. He was often late and often full of silly excuses that turned out to be the truth. But his excuses were sober and reasonable this time and a pack of lies.

Chapter Fourteen

At home a few evenings later, on a rare night alone, Mike and Susannah sat in the library (red leather, rainbow chintz, dark paneling, more bastard Cherryhill). The dinner trays had been removed, and each was relaxing in his and her way, he watching Milton Berle on TV, she reading a novel, a story she could have written better herself but one which made her think about youth and age, the passing of years, younger women.

"Mike?"

"What?"

"Turn the sound down. I want to ask you something. What's up with Di? Every time I look around, I see the two of you talking to each other as if you'd both lost your last friend, or were planning to assassinate someone."

"I've been trying to talk some sense into her."

"Such as?"

"Pointing out that with three little kids, that huge place, the whole way of life, and not that much money, they ought to get back together." She noticed at his throat a telltale pulse, quickening. A lie detector wouldn't miss that pulse.

"And all those dogs, too. I've always wondered who gets the dogs. But is it up to her?"

"Sure it's up to her."

"What about the blonde?"

"She'll get rid of the blonde. Living with Jack, that's like getting rid of roaches in a city kitchen. You just keep calling the exterminator." Then, after a pause: "I don't believe in divorce."

"That's good news," determined to keep it light.

"Especially when there are kids," he added, foolishly, unnecessarily, turning the TV back up.

"Mike?"

"*What?* That book's not grabbing you. Try something else."

"Will you turn that off, please? I want to talk to you about something. We never talk anymore. You talk to everyone, it seems, except to me."

"Maybe that's because talking to you means *you talk*. Look, I've had a rough day."

"Tell me about your rough day. I'm not dumb. I can understand about things like the SEC and Dow Jones and buying on margin and selling short and mutual funds . . . I've read books."

A laugh. Not his most friendly laugh. "It's not all in books, Susannah. When are you going to learn that?"

"I'm interested."

"You never used to be interested. Anyhow, I don't want to talk. I want to watch the TV."

"Then *I'll* talk. Because *I've* had a rough day. I got my period again. I'm so disappointed I could cry. Do you think there's something wrong with me?"

"Only everything."

"Be serious. It's been six months now that I haven't used anything and I'm still not pregnant."

"Give it time."

"They say if you use birth control for too many years, then sometimes you can't ever get pregnant." She came over and sat beside him on the arm of his chair.

"That sounds straight from the mouth of my mother, the horse. Go get checked out. Anyhow, what's the rush? A long time ago, when I was young and foolish, and didn't have much else to do or think about, I wanted us to have a kid right away, remember?"

"I remember."

"I was real curious about Mike, Jr., what he'd be like. I thought that would be real nice, for us to have a kid. And you said . . ."

"I know. I *know.*" She realized she was doing something he hated, peeling the scarlet varnish off her nails. But she couldn't stop, wanting to punish herself for the stupid, careless fashion in which she'd snubbed those sweet urgent feelings he'd once had about her, tender shoots of feelings that seemed to have been killed by an unseasonable frost. They were "the Brownes" now, leaders of "the Squad," but where were Mike and Susannah, Mick and Slick?

"Actually," he said, after awhile, as if he'd been giving the matter serious thought, his arm casually around her, "it wouldn't be so great now, would it? I mean what would that do to next summer, if you got knocked up?" They had vast plans for the summer of 1950, which would simultaneously accommodate his recurring need to risk life and limb, hers to sight-see and meet famous people.

"It's never convenient to have a baby," she said, which was

exactly what he used to say to her only a couple of years earlier.

"Still," he said casually, but the voice wasn't one you lightly ignored, "let's put it off till after the summer. O.K.? You go back to the old rubber monocle, like a good girl."

"Not O.K. I don't like you."

"That's an order, Slick. No funny business."

"Maybe no business at all . . ." She'd done both thumbs now, filling an ashtray with red shavings, and began on a forefinger.

"Will you stop that," he said suddenly, very loudly. "Please *stop doing that.*"

In his voice she could hear strained nerves, a hint of disgust, and something else; a note of fear, protest, a refusal to be trapped. His voice was her voice, long ago, with someone she wanted, suddenly, to shuck off and be rid of.

"Don't take it out on me," she said now to Mike Browne. "Whatever it is."

Chapter Fifteen

How banal and ordinary are the particulars of a wife's observation that her husband is falling in love with someone else. For a long while there is nothing to define. Only that wherever he is, she, the interloper, is; wherever she is, he is. Whatever she's doing, whether standing by a fire or at a bar, smoking in a theater lobby or bicycling down a country road, or playing ball in Central Park of a Sunday morning, he is doing it, too. At dinner parties they always seem to be seated next to each other. After dinner, if there's music, if Claude Rust, everybody's favorite piano player, has shown up to entertain, you can be sure to find them hanging over the piano, and sooner or later one of them will ask for the song that appears to be theirs: the one about snow snowing, wind blowing, icicles forming, and love warming.

Susannah would have loved to drive an icicle into the heart of Diana Weatherby, whose hair was a red cloud, who had taken to wearing bright colors, but her friend Kitty, whose speciality was illicit romance, had given her the word: Ignore it. If you ignore it, it will go away, unlike cancer.

So she ignored it. She walked into a ski lodge on New Year's weekend, a safe place in Vermont since Diana preferred Canada, but this year: surprise, there foxface was. And bright and early the next morning Mike and Di were off in a group to the tows while Susannah and Kitty Jones, the ski widows, sleepers and readers who only did a little ice skating (both of them suffered vertigo, feared speed, hated cold), the orchid and the hothouse rose, stayed behind, killing the day until the *après* ski. Only this holiday, the *après* ski did not center around the bright conversation and sexiness of lazy Susannah and sleepy Kitty. It revolved around sporty Di Weatherby, in old pants and a ratty sweater, her hair a fiery halo, talking in her husky movie star voice with the men, about other slopes, snow conditions, and finally shooing everyone off to bed early.

A few weeks later the Brownes got off a plane, into a blast of warm air, brilliant sun, azure skies, and, surprise, there Di was again, already deeply tanned, in shorts and bandanna, arrived a day or so earlier. The next morning, down they went, Mike and Di, off the side of a cabin cruiser in masks and flippers, armed with spears, while Kitty and Susannah sunned on a deck (being both of them claustrophobes, terrified of depths). "You oughtta work up nerve," he'd said to Susannah long ago. "I have nerve," she'd said. "It's called 'some nerve.'" Her kind of nerve had opened doors wherever they went. Once he'd enjoyed lunching with Lord Beaverbrook in Nassau, dining with Somerset Maugham in Cap Ferrat. Once her kind of nerve had kept him entertained. Now it left him indifferent.

A few weeks after that he said, "Diana's been talking about next summer. If she can get her divorce out of the way, she's thinking of taking the kids to Switzerland. We might share a house. I've always wanted to do the Eiger."

"And what will I do, while you're doing the Eiger?"

"Whatever you usually do, talk to artists and writers, read, sight-see."

"There's no sightseeing in Switzerland, and no artists or writers. I thought we were going to Africa. I thought you were talking Di out of her divorce. You certainly spend enough time talking, the two of you."

"Oh, she's a stubborn woman," he said, "almost as stubborn as you are," grinning, trying to be charming, and she wanted to wipe the grin off his face with steel wool.

But nobody says anything. No one is caught doing anything. It's all frightfully civilized. When there has been no real danger, Susannah has pulled all kinds of tricks: she has spilled crème de menthe on his boiled shirt for paying too much attention to some blonde. She has thrown glasses of champagne. She has given way to all sorts of unusual rages and tried to throw his saddle out the window. Now, faced with real danger she has been very, very quiet.

"These things don't happen overnight," he said later, cruelly.

"We did," she said. "We happened overnight." But he looked blank as if he had forgotten, as if he could not imagine it happening any other way than imperceptibly, two old acquaintances who have known each other all their lives, becoming, unexpectedly, "terrific friends."

That's how Diane put it to Susannah one day at lunch. "Funny," she said to Susannah, "how you can know someone like Mike all your life and not know him at all, then in one year become such *terrific friends*. He's been so great about all my problems. And God, he makes me laugh."

But the two old acquaintances, recently become such "terrific friends," had clearly stopped laughing long enough to get into bed, somewhere along the way, and after the first time they had perhaps been cheerful, casual and appropriately off-hand, as "terrific friends" should be: no strings. Perhaps they'd even said that it must never happen again. Except naturally it has happened again.

Thus Susannah imagined the progress of the addiction. "Ignore it," Kitty told her. "The fun of these things for him, I swear it, is to get a rise out of you. It's surely not the first time."

"For all the kidding around," Susannah said to her friend, "I believe it is."

Then all hell broke loose. He wanted Diana to take him seriously and he no longer needed or wanted to be taken seriously by Susannah.

One fine spring day, quite coolly, Mike brought Diana out to Cherryhill for good old Sunday lunch, at almost precisely the same time of year he'd first brought Susannah there, four years earlier. A final bit of treachery. That was the day Susannah couldn't stand it anymore, the day she stopped being civilized because she was frightened.

"Why is *she* coming?" Susannah asked that morning.

"I guess mother needs a pretty girl."

Pretty was she now, old foxface?

All the way out in the car Di and Susannah talked furiously about some burning issue (May, 1950: Joe McCarthy? Syngman Rhee? More likely Rita Hayworth and Aly Khan, would their marriage last?). Mike remained silent and looked angry, as if the women's chatter were getting on his nerves. He wasn't even especially friendly to Diana, his terrific friend, regretting perhaps the close quarters of this expedition. "Do you think you two know what you're talking about?" was all he said. Susannah never caught him looking at Diana who sat between them seductively dressed in a new pastel suit. She could only see Diana watching him, staring not at his face, but at his hands and wrists at the wheel, at the big gold ring on his little finger, at the center stone glittering. They seemed to fascinate her, those strong weathered hands.

"Some things are too personal," Susannah said suddenly, apropos of something they'd been discussing.

"Like?" asked Di.

"Sex, for instance. Death. A dead person's clothing. Someone else's toothbrush. Someone else's sheets. Someone else's diaphragm."

"You think of such *things*," said Diana.

Mike said nothing, just tightened.

At lunch, a large and gala affair, Susannah was ready to jump out of her own pretty pastel suit, right out of her skin. She was not up to the company that was laughing and drinking on Violet's terrace. There was a duchess from Paris and her small vibrant husband who looked like a figure in a tapestry. There was a chinless English wonder, cousin to the royal family, and his bleating bride, whose honeymoon trip proved to be the reason for the lunch. Another fancy Britisher, with a chin like a headsman's ax and savage blue eyes, had two words at his command, "bloody" and "boring." ("So boring to talk about," he kept saying to Susannah, on his right at lunch, whatever topic she'd bring up, though to Diana on his left he kept saying, "Bloody good, that, bloody jolly, that.") There were some members of U.S. royalty, a famous statesman, a magazine tycoon and his icy, glamorous wife who wrote plays, and a liver-spotted man in a loud checked suit who was the fifth richest man (by the latest *Fortune* poll) in America.

Once upon a time, the new Mrs. Michael Browne might have felt awed by such company, would have suffered rudenesses, trying too hard and getting snubbed for her pains. Later, more sure of herself, she would have been amused to exert her wiles at least on the males of such company and (to the irritation of the women) make a few conquests. Now she neither suffered rudenesses nor exerted wiles, but simply waited for the proverbial last straw, which was gallantly presented to her, after lunch, by the tiny Duke.

Everyone was on the terrace, breathing the sweet air, holding up faces to golden afternoon sun. Mike, inevitably, gravitated to Diana who took puffs of his cigar. Sitting side by side on a wall, neither of them saying much, they looked peaceful, domestic, and superior to their surroundings as if they belonged together. Standing next to Susannah, Monsieur le Duc, trying to make conversation, said, "So stupid one is about names. You are, please, Diana?"

"No. Susannah."

"Ah yes. One is also stupid about who goes with who. Now that one over there," pointing to the liver-spotted money bags, "someone told me that was your husband."

"No. *That's* my husband," pointing to Mike, who sat in the sun smiling at Diana, hair flopping over his noble furrowed brow: *mine*.

"Ah. I thought he was married to her," pointing to Diana.

"No. She has no husband. At present."

Then Violet, having heard, rushed in to smooth things over, began talking about her trees and recalling to Susannah the first time she had ever come to Cherryhill.

"Their real anniversary is in July," she said to the tiny Duke, putting her arm around Susannah's waist. "But I always think of their anniversary as May, the first time this dear child came to see me."

That was the moment Susannah excused herself and ran through the house, down the steps, into the car.

Screeching through the gate out onto the road, almost losing control of the car because, though she'd finally got her license, she wasn't much of a driver, Susannah thought: "He'll be sorry; he'll realize how precious I was." Then she thought, "maybe not, maybe that's just what he'd love, to get me out of the way," and drove very carefully, very accurately, back into town.

The phone began ringing a few minutes after she reached the apartment. She let it ring.

Chapter Sixteen

Mike arrived home furious: how could she have pulled something like that? Taken his car, no message, no good-by, leaving him stranded, worrying the life out of him with visions of her bloody on the highway.

Sitting on the bed, surrounded by a mess of Sunday papers, overflowing ashtrays, empty cups and glasses, also a half empty jar of Skippy's peanut butter and a box of saltines, she let him have it: weeks and months worth of stored-up recriminations. He sat silent, till she came to the heart, till she shrieked out the name.

"I didn't think you went for red-haired bitches with no front, but now I know. I've seen her look at you. I know that look . . . oh, say something!"

He stared at her without expression, saying nothing. Her

voice rose, though she remained sitting cross-legged on the bed. "I can understand her wanting to fuck you, because you're very good at it. It's one of the things you do best. What I don't understand is why she comes to my house, why she rides in my car, why she pretends to be my friend. And you, you two-faced lying coward . . ."

She slapped him.

In the years they had known each other she had made other less direct gestures, exotic and imaginative expressions of rage. But she had never taken her hand, thus, and applied it to his face, hard, so it left a red mark on his cheek and stung her palm.

In a low angry voice, he said: "I don't have to take that from you."

"Are you having an affair with her?"

"That's none of your business."

Then he said, "If I'm so terrible, why don't you divorce me?"

"I'd love to. Five thousand a week alimony and ten million in cash. That should keep me in the style to which you've accustomed me. I'll take the apartment and the furniture. You can have the family portraits and the silver."

"I'm serious, Susannah," he said very quietly. "If I'm such a bastard, and I'm making you so unhappy, let's finish it. I'm sure something reasonable can be worked out. I'm not stingy."

"I'm serious, too." Her voice lowered. "If you want a divorce you'll pay for it, in every way."

The scene was not following the rules. He should have been concerned and solicitous, anything but what he was: waxy, artificial, a store dummy with opaque blue eyes.

"Are you calling my bluff, Mick?" It was she who was concerned, solicitous. "I got carried away. You know me, though. I store it up."

"I'm not calling your bluff. I think we've had it."

Then terror. Nothing was different in his face, but something in his eyes had changed. The jaw had set.

"Don't *look* like that. Don't *say* things like that. *Had what?* I was joking. I'd never give you a divorce, not for ten million dollars."

"Everyone has his price."

"Not me. I'm priceless."

Then she began to cry, great racking sobs, and he had to hold her.

"I can always get an annulment," he said gravely, when she'd calmed down.

"On what grounds? Insanity? Epilepsy? Bigamy? Inability to consummate the marriage? Hah!"

"Drunkenness. That's grounds. Total inebriation. Your Honor, she had me so intoxicated, so completely drunk on her at the time of our marriage, sir, I didn't know what I was doing."

"Were you really worried about me this afternoon?" she asked.

"Yes."

"Would you be sorry if I was dead?"

"Yes."

He put her back down on the bed, onto Sunday papers that crackled beneath her. "You did, you know, get me drunk, stoned out of my mind, Miss Rose . . ." he said, and lay down beside her.

"Last night you didn't want me," she protested. "You couldn't even get it up. Why now? I don't feel like it."

"Maybe I didn't want you last night. Ever think of that?" he said, wanting her now, aroused by the quarrel, by her flushed face and ripe flesh and tangled hair. "Hey," he said, remembering.

"It's all right," she said, lying as easily as he lied. "I'm safe."

He took her quickly, in sudden lust, atop the Sunday papers, as if she were some stranger, and made her come, in spite of herself, and come again, made her beg and moan.

"Are you still Mick?" she asked afterward, languishing on the faces of Harry Truman, Joe McCarthy, Josef Stalin.

"I guess so."

"Well, then you still love Susannah. Don't you?"

"If you say so."

"*You* say so. You never say so anymore."

"IloveyouIloveyouIloveyouIloveyouloveyouloveyaloveyaluvlalavalvla . . ." he said faster and faster till the sounds became meaningless, a demented tongue twister. And of all the times they'd made love, this time, in limbo, bore fruit.

A few weeks later Mike told Susannah that he wanted a divorce. He wanted to move out that evening. "I'm in love with Diana," he said. "You knew before I did. You know so much."

Through the great glass window of the living room a dramatic sunset was in progress, staining everything red. Over the fireplace the famous Mexican's portrait of her seemed about to burst into flames.

"I tried to tell you on that Sunday," he said.

"Instead you made love to me. Why?"

"Because when I fight with you I get horny."

"O.K., let's fight."

"Anyhow, I didn't make love to you that night. I fucked you."

"Isn't that the same thing? Aren't great fucks what love is all about? And see, it's pretty funny . . ." She stopped. She couldn't say it, not now.

"There's no nice way to tell you this," he said.

"Nice people lose out. Remember?"

"I want to marry her."

"You're married to me," she said. "I'm *your wife.*" The enormity of what he had told her eluded her. Stupidly, she recalled there was something she was going to tell him, but that was lost.

"I've never been married to you," he said. "That's the problem. I've never felt married to you. We've been something else, a love affair, something you go into with crossed fingers."

"I felt married to you."

"We are two people with nothing in common, not one thing we share, when you come down to it, but ourselves. Maybe if we'd had a kid . . ."

Then she remembered what she was going to say and again didn't say it. She said: "It seemed to me we had a lot in common, a lot of things shared. Right here in this apartment we're surrounded with souvenirs of things we've shared, a lot of jokes, a lot of tears, a lot of very real feelings."

"What can I say?"

"But to you none of it was *real*. You say I was never married to you, and you realized this the week of Gussie's funeral." Her voice was bitter. "You felt *real* talking to Diana Weatherby. Like you were waking up from a long drunken sleep, just like you said, because she's right—she's what you were programed to love—but I'm wrong and nothing on earth is ever going to change that."

"I don't know what you're talking about," he said wearily. "Just listening to you makes me feel like an old man. You're too much for a simple character like me. You need someone brilliant, with a big brain. You need to get back to thinking and writing. You must be bored, if you'd just admit it. I'm not good enough for you."

"You're just suffering from a temporary derangement. Some sort of stupid *reflex*. *You* will be so bored with that woman."

"Our relationship is dead, Susannah."

"Not *quite*," she said, finally. "Guess what?"

As she told him when and where and how, he looked at her with frank hatred. "I don't believe you," he said flatly. "I'm leaving." And without stopping to pack, he left the apartment.

The next afternoon Peter Plainfield came to pack a bag and a brief case and took the luggage away to one of Mike's many clubs, where he was staying until matters were settled.

Susannah was in the living room when Pete arrived. She looked at him unflinching with what he once called her big Old Testament eyes, but she didn't speak.

After he left, though, she began throwing crockery, glassware, certain she would lose the baby because how could she be so upset and not miscarry?

But all that happened was that she cut her foot quite deeply on broken glass and had to bandage herself clumsily. All night long the damn thing kept opening, soaking the sheets red.

Then, more quietly and sensibly, she said to herself: *he can't do this to me.*

Chapter Seventeen

The next day Susannah went to see Violet.

She came upon her mother-in-law in the cutting garden of Cherryhill, with her basket and scissors, gardening gloves on her hands, racy hat on her head, a comical air about her. She reminded Susannah of the friendly neighborhood eccentric in the children's book who turns out to be a witch, still friendly, but able to work spells.

"Well, Susannah, what a nice surprise! Why didn't you call?" A soft cheek brushed hers. Whiffs of Mary Chess Lilac and tobacco assailed her. "What is it, dear girl? You look terrible. Here, hold this . . ." handing her the basket, piled with blossoms. "I'll be one minute. Such terrible thorns," finishing a delicate operation in a scarlet rose bush. "Then we'll have a cup of tea."

"In Eden the roses didn't have any thorns," Susannah said.

On the warm bright terrace, where the two women had first crossed swords and made friends, Susannah told Violet, with little censoring, what had transpired, pausing in her narrative only once, on Violet's signal, when Hanley came with the tea things (that was a lesson she'd never learned, to Violet's exasperation: never talk in front of servants, children, and taxi drivers). Violet nodded, listened, calm and self-possessed, full of Olympian serenity, in back of which the old brain was ticking away. Her color came up, her eyes snapped, because there was nothing like a crisis to put new life into Violet Browne.

"Where is my son at this moment?" asked Violet, breaking a long silence. "With her?"

"They're not that dumb. She's working things out with Jack Weatherby. He's at one of his stupid clubs."

"That's not stupid, my dear. Thank God for clubs. Sometimes I think you make a mistake thinking so many of the things he enjoys are stupid. But for the moment let's not talk about my son. Let's talk about you. What do you want?"

"I don't know."

"Things can be arranged, of course."

"You're telling me? If you're rich you can always arrange a safe abortion," watching with satisfaction Violet's wince. "I want the baby."

"Good. I'm glad."

"You are?"

"Did you think I might tell you to be sensible? Buy you off? Because you think Diana's what I wanted for him in the first place?"

"Something like that."

"No, you didn't or you wouldn't be here. I've known Diana Weatherby all her life. She means well. She's always had a yen for Mike, poor dear, but she's a slob. You are an original. I admire you. You've worked miracles with my son. Besides, you make me laugh."

Patronizing old bitch, Susannah thought. But never mind. She's thinking. And that's good for me and bad for him.

"You want the baby. Next question: do you want your husband back?"

"I don't think you understand. He's left me."

"I know my son. I know the sort of person he is. I imagine at this moment he's already regretting what he's done and said."

"He said he loves her. What he's done I don't believe he regrets at all. The question now is only money: just money. How much can I get, for myself and my child." How could she express to his mother, on this bright protected terrace, the loathing she felt, the contempt, the fury of a woman ditched.

Susannah stood up and began to pace.

"Sit down," said Violet smiling. "I'm on your side. He's my son, but I've always run the wives' union. Wandering is one thing, abandonment another. Obviously I'd choose to avoid a scandal. But the important thing is, again, what do you want? War? Revenge? A new life? Your old life as a writer back? Another man? Money? Or do you want to save your marriage?"

"He says we never had a marriage."

"That's what they all say. Anyhow, it's you that we're talking about." Violet lit a cigarette, blew three perfect smoke rings, like the Camel sign in Times Square. "I'm reminded of a friend of mine, a lovely woman, who years ago sued her husband for divorce in New York on the grounds of adultery. He had a mistress—not the first—and his wife found out. In the end he'd wanted to come back, not just for the sake of the children, but for her. And my friend wanted to take him back, but her *pride* would not allow her to do anything else but go through with the divorce. She felt she should be so angry that she could no longer live with him. That if she forgave him she could not live with herself, or rather the picture she had of herself. Do you follow me? She was the proudest, most unhappy woman I ever knew."

"And you're saying?"

"Try to sort out what you really feel as opposed to what you think you *should* feel."

"Right now I feel like throwing up. It hits me every afternoon."

"Why don't you lie down." Violet looked at her watch and got up from the long chair where for almost two hours she had been reposing while Susannah had twisted and squirmed and paced. "I wish I weren't going out tonight. I'd ask you to stay and have dinner with me. Would you stay anyhow? Get a good night's sleep. We can talk again in the morning."

She never made any physical gestures toward other people, except her children. Still, she touched her daughter-in-law's tumbled hair shyly, then took her daughter-in-law's face in her two hands and smoothed the furrowed forehead and said, "I want to help you."

"You're very kind," said Susannah, almost seeing a mother's face, almost placing her trust in another woman.

Was Violet kind? Or getting her own back. As once her son had loved to bug and thwart her, was she now fixing her son?

"Tell me something," said Violet the next morning in the rose garden, as she clipped and pruned, while Susannah held the basket. "Tell me, if you knew you would never see him again, knew you'd have a perfectly good life but he would be absent forever from it, dead or on the other side of the earth, how would you feel?"

In different ways, Violet had questioned and speculated, moved on and off the subject, always returning to the central issue, not what the man felt and wanted, but what the woman felt and wanted, because once that was clear, then they could proceed.

"I'd survive."

Silence.

"I'd feel I'd never be young again, I'd never be excited

again, really excited, but I'd never be snubbed again, either."

Violet remained silent, going about her gardening as if she hadn't heard.

"All *right,*" Susannah said, finally, throwing down the basket, scattering the roses. "All right. Some day it may come back at both of us, but yes, to hell with pride, I want him back. But I want him back the right way, if he comes back for *me,* Susannah, not for the child, not for some antique gentleman's sense of honor, for *me* . . ."

"Then get a lawyer," said Violet, the old campaigner, the manipulator of people and lives, who believed that anything could be arranged and achieved, if you went about it the right way. Violet was boss of the wives' union, the women's underground, and more important, she held the purse strings.

Chapter Eighteen

The phone in Susannah's bedroom rang. She answered.

"Hello. Susannah?"

"Who's this?"

"Mike."

"Yes, Mike."

"I want to see you."

"Why?"

"I want to talk to you about some things."

"Talk to my lawyer."

"I've talked to your lawyer. My lawyer has talked to your lawyer. I've read through that proposed agreement. It's longer than the Constitution and even less clear. There are things you and I have to discuss. Some of what you're asking for is simply not possible. There are other things you should be asking for that you aren't."

"Nothing that can't be discussed by the lawyers," she said.

"Did you read my letter?"

"Yes, I read your fucking letter."

"You didn't answer it. You took it the wrong way."

"There was no right way to take it."

"I wrote you again."

"I gave that one to my lawyer. I didn't read it."

"I want to see you," he said.

"I don't want to see you. I would find it much too upsetting to see you. Good-by."

Bang.

"Susannah, it's bad manners to hang up on people."

"I don't have any manners. I *don't* want to talk to you."

"Sooner or later you'll have to talk to me, with the lawyers or without. I'd rather talk to you alone."

"Mike, face it. I'll see you in court."

"What's that mean?"

"What I say. If things don't get worked out quietly, we can settle them in court."

"Don't talk nonsense."

"I'm not talking nonsense."

"I want to do the right thing for you. You're making it very difficult. Diana and I both . . ."

"Shut up. Sign the agreement, that's all. As we've drawn it up."

"That's impossible. You're not being reasonable. Susannah, don't hang up. Wait."

"*What?*"

"Do you need anything? Is everything all right?"

"You mean, am I holding on to the baby? Yes. That baby must want to be born. Good-by."

"I'm going out of town. I'll call you back next week when you're in a better mood."

Then:

"Susannah?"

"Yes, Mike."

"I'm going to try to work out the money. Did the lawyer tell you?"

"Yes."

"Now I want to see you. Concerning the timing of the divorce. And the child. My rights as the father of this child."

"You have no rights, Mike. I could sue you right here in New York State, and give you spades, and win."

"I doubt that. Anyhow, I'm coming to see you. My lawyer wants me to. What's the matter? Are you afraid to see me?"

"Hell, no. But my doctor has forbidden me to see you. Also my psychiatrist, my dentist, and my hairdresser."

"You're being so tough, baby, and I want to do the right thing for once in my life. I want to set things up for you in the best possible way. Why won't you give me a chance to say what I have to say?"

"Say it now. Spit it out," she said.

"I want to say it in person."

"Nothing you have to say could interest me. You want to get rid of your guilt. You're not going to get rid of it seeing me."

"You hate me, don't you?"

"No. I don't feel anything except a slight impatience."

"I don't believe that. You've never felt anything slight in your life."

"However, my doctor says I hate you. A lot. He says I just haven't caught up with it. You're being a pain, Mike."

"Tell me one thing: what do you look like? Are you fat?"

"I'm very thin. So long, Mike."

Then:

"You listen to me now, Susannah. I went to see my mother today."

"I love your mother."

"I went to see my mother to check some things out. Because what you're asking for adds up to what I don't have. Not the way you want it. Not right now. Even if I wanted to give it to you. And mother said she'd advised you to make sure of certain things for you and the baby, but she agrees this is totally unreasonable. She said: 'I can't go along with this. I think Susannah is hysterical. Pregnancy does that to some women. Pregnancy combined with a shock.'"

"I'm not in the least hysterical."

"Mother said: 'talk to her, that's the only thing to do. I'll talk to her, also.'"

"So Mummy won't pay up. Well, I'll see you in court then."

"You are a flip bitch. I'd like to . . ."

"What, Mike? What would you like to do? The relationship is dead, remember? I don't exist, except on paper. Let's keep it that way. I have to go now. I'm late for dinner."

Bang.

And so on.

Thus Violet and Susannah played him like a fish, let him wear himself out, let his mistress, the poor freckled-faced mother of three and wife of none, nag him from the other end and not so gracefully under pressure. "I expect that girl will not know how to handle him," Violet had said. "I expect they'll run their course."

Chapter Nineteen

"You can believe it because I'm telling you, and you know your girl friend." Red Jones, society wine dealer and deposed husband of Kitty, was pouring out his heart, half kidding, to Susannah Browne, society bright girl and deposed wife of Mike. He was swirling brandy in a snifter, she was sipping creme de menthe. The two of them sat back in plush chairs under the pink clouds of the St. Regis roof. Bouncy music played. All of their friends would have sworn it was impossible that those two should be amicably spending an evening together, but in the city summer breeds odd friendships. Comrades in misery, they'd run into each other one evening at the Plaza Theater, each alone and hiding, went to supper afterward to talk about the film and presently about themselves and their perfidious absent spouses. They amused and consoled each other and had repeated the process several times since.

"Can you imagine it, Susie?" he continued. She hadn't cured him of calling her Susie, Susie Q, Lazy Susan. "The house in the middle of the finest vineyard in France, the guests, everyone ready to go into dinner, waiting for my sweet wife. We'd never stayed in such a house before. I admit I was impressed. I told her so."

"Mistake."

"I admit it. I told her what I wanted her to wear, and what she should say . . . or not say . . . and that on no account could she smoke before or during dinner."

"Worse mistake."

"So everyone was ready to go into the dining room . . ." his voice was light but sexy. (The best thing about him, Kitty always said. "That voice pours over me," she said, "like chocolate sauce on vanilla ice cream.") "And then she appeared, your friend, our Kitty, walking down the stairs, and she was wearing nothing, absolutely nothing but a purple bikini and her mother's pearls. 'Oh,' she said, 'I thought we were going to tread the grapes.' "

They both began to laugh. He had a nice face when he laughed, not a sleek red seal anymore but a fresh kid.

"Sure it's funny if you're not married to it. What was she punishing me for, over and over?" he said. "For marrying her? Why did she do it?"

"I asked her once. She said, 'Why does any girl get married at nineteen? The body says, *allons-y,* and besides, how else do you get away from mother?' Listen, I think she's punishing you for not being someone else."

"Someone before me?" he asked.

"Maybe. Maybe someone in her mind who doesn't exist."

"It's not so funny, either, sometimes. She can be destructive . . ." He was off again, telling all the old stories, the ones that didn't involve the current heart of the matter, the playboy polo player Larky Harrison with whom at this very moment Kitty was no doubt passing the time in Monte Carlo.

"What would *you* have done?" Red was asking. "Locked her up?"

Who? What? Fingers snapped at her. "Hey, sleepy Sue, where are you? I'm trying to take your mind off your troubles by involving you in mine." Big grin, hand closed for a moment over hers. "Where the hell are you tonight?"

"Mike called again."

"Why doesn't he leave you alone and get on with it?"

"That's what I say. He really seems to want to see me."

"He wants to make himself feel better, that's all. He wants you to absolve him from feeling like a dog. Don't see him."

"Have you seen him?"

"Sure."

"And?"

"Nothing. He's a very old friend. We don't always agree on things."

"I think I have to see him, Red. I've stopped hurting so much thanks partly to you. And I know I'll live, also partly thanks to you. Still, I think I would like to handle this in a generous way." She smiled. He frowned. He didn't want to talk about Mike Browne. He had a different plan for this evening. "I think I owe that, not to him, but to myself," she said.

"You owe yourself something else. To hell with him. Come on. Let's go."

"You're going to take me home so early? I thought we were night owls."

"I'm going to take you home to my place." Not smiling, his brows slightly raised he looked halfway between seal and pumpkin. Asking something.

"No."

"Why?"

"For one reason, he's got a tail on me."

"Better reason."

"I'm pregnant."

"Not noticeably. Still better reason?"

"I have to get things straight with Mike. In some addled way he wants us to stay friends, for the sake of the child. Of course we can't be friends, but on the other hand I want to reassure him that what I'm filled with is *pity*, for both of us . . . for what we were . . ."

"Crap." All seal now, he snapped his fingers for the waiter. Among the things she didn't find so charming about him were those snapping fingers, the way he handled waiters, taxi drivers, salesgirls, doormen. "What are you trying to say?" Red Jones asked.

"I think I still love him," she said. "I didn't know till right now. I feel like a fool."

"You *are* a fool." He grinned. His grin was notable. Couldn't match Mike Browne's, though.

As she let herself into the apartment she noticed the living room lights were on, the study was a rosy glow, and the door to the terrace was wide open. For a second she was terrified. Then she remembered the peculiar expression on the face of the night elevator man and understood.

"How the hell did you get in?" she asked. "I've changed the locks."

"I climbed up," said he, who did not mishandle waiters, taxi drivers, elevator men, who from birth had had his ways of twisting such people to his needs. In a Charles Boyer voice he said, "May I introduce myself, Lady Susannah, Michel, the human fly."

"Climb right back down."

"You *are* thin." His own deep, snotty voice now, once thrilling to her. "That's not good for the kid."

"Get *out*."

"Speaking of out, where've you been till this hour?"

"*Out*."

"Who with?"

"Wait for tomorrow's report. That's pretty low, tailing a pregnant woman."

"You're not any old pregnant woman. Really, you look terrific."

"I'm calling the police." She went into the living room and began to dial, but quick as a burglar he was behind her, taking the receiver from her. She stared at him and thought how corny his handsomeness was. Why had she ever thought him a work of art when he was only a billboard, a theatrical ad? And how flashy and inappropriate his matinee idol stance. She felt as if her brains were overcooked; I don't hate him, but I don't love him anymore. That was one more pose, that breathless confession under the pink clouds of the St. Regis roof. He is nothing to me. There is no connection between him and the baby growing in my womb.

The thought filled her with terror: this Celluloid man was her gravity, and if she didn't have that, what was she other than a balloon floating off into space.

"Susannah." He was staring at her in a way that made her angry and sad and confused. "Can I talk to you. For ten minutes. No more. Please?" She'd never heard him say please before, except as an oath: pu-*leeze*.

"All right, ten minutes. Someone is going to tell me this is stupid."

They sat face to face, each in a big square chair, formally, like sculptures.

"Life is never simple," he began. "You can think you want one thing more than anything in the world, you can think you want to be rid of something else more than anything in the world . . ."

"Some*one*, Mike. Try to be precise."

"Some*one*. Then, a thing happens you hadn't bargained on. At first it means nothing. Only makes you angry. You refuse to acknowledge . . ." Pause. He was flip and glib on a surface level, handy with words, but clumsy when serious. She wasn't going to help him. "After awhile," he continued, "this thing that's happened gets to you. It got to me after awhile that you were having a baby. My baby. I'm responsible. I want you to have everything you need. I *care* what happens to you."

"The last time we sat in this room I could see how tremendously you cared."

"You were playing games. You didn't tell me straight off."

"When was I going to tell you? After you'd said, hey, old dear, I want a divorce, or gee honey, you and I have never been married, or gosh sweets, it isn't as if we had children . . . ?"

"Before that night. Before you went to the doctor. Before I'd said anything."

"Then what? Gun to your head? Have you go all noble, remembering your classy upbringing, back to Diana to say, dearest love, I cannot desert her now . . . *Shit.* What's the point of this. Why are you here?"

"Susannah!" Again that demanding, directing look, blue as the heart of a flame, that was making her intensely uncomfortable. "The world could be coming to an end and you'd fall right into the old patterns. Listen, whether you're married to me or not, you are Mrs. Browne. And for Mrs. Browne, this agreement you've had drawn up is insane. And if I don't sign it, you're going to haul me into court, here in New York? Bullshit."

"Not bullshit."

"On what grounds?"

"Adultery."

"The courts don't take as evidence hearsay or putting two and two together. Your lawyer must have told you that."

"He did. I have evidence." He was back to normal now, on the attack, which made her feel better. She couldn't resist a wise guy smile.

"Not possible. I haven't seen Diana except in full public view, since I left you."

"I know." A savoring pause. "I had you followed for that entire month between our delightful Sunday at Cherryhill and the night it was good-by forever. I had you tailed, chump. You thought you were invisible. No flash bulb, no final photo, but believe me enough words, names, places, to nail you and your sweet friend . . ."

This was the moment for him to walk out, stop wavering. Instead he began to laugh.

"You think that's funny?"

"I have to hand it to you," still laughing.

"You are ridiculous," she said to this man she didn't know.

Her chance was now; his chance was now; their chance was now, but slipping away as something, in spite of them, began to take hold.

"*We're* ridiculous."

"Ten minutes are more than up, Mike," looking at her watch, the one he'd given her. They both stood.

"I see you're still wearing that. And the clips. But you're not wearing your ring."

"The ring's gone."

"How much did you get for it? It belonged to my mother."

"I didn't sell it. I flushed it down the john."

"That's an expensive and hostile gesture." She could tell she'd hit home with that one.

"Speaking of rings, where's yours?" She'd sensed something missing, for some minutes, a part of his person incomplete. That was it. The naked little finger of his right hand. "I thought you never took it off. I thought you'd die if you took it off?"

"I'm grown up now."

"Where is it?"

"I don't think you want to know." So Di had it. Her hands

were big enough to carry it off. He'd hit home with that one, no question.

"I'm not clear," she said, "about what you wanted to tell me about the agreement. You have some suggestions about money. And the child."

He inclined his head. Very lordly.

"It's late," she said.

"Can I come back tomorrow? Alone. No lawyer."

It's her turn to nod. Very gracious lady.

In morning brightness they sat in the ruby den, on either side of the stately eighteenth-century desk. He had brought with him a folder of papers and proffered a plan for money, trusts, and taxes. It was a generous plan. In return he asked only for certain rights concerning the child. He expressed his willingness, indeed his desire, to postpone proceedings until after the child was born.

She listened to what he had to say in silence, waiting for what she expected would come, conscious of the fact that she was looking well, at almost thirty-three could still take morning light, conscious of the effect of blue black hair, green eyes, lashes, tender line of cheek, soft throat on the man opposite her. Presently he said: "There's another possibility. We could try to get back together again."

Silence.

"I found it wasn't so easy, after all, to throw out four years."

"That's a rotten idea," she said after awhile. "How long have you had that rotten idea?"

"About twelve hours."

"What about Diana?"

"Let's not talk about her. That's my problem."

"She must be almost ready to leave Reno now, with her divorce and everything."

"I said that's my problem."

"So she bored you. Poor Mick."

"She didn't bore me. She was lovely."

"I don't accept your sacrifice."

"Be humble, Susannah. Try."

"Humble! Don't give me that crap. Don't move," pushing back her chair, moving back away from the hands stretched out to her, from the quick smile—not a grin—a true honest smile. "Don't *touch* me. When I think of all that bullshit you handed out to me."

"And you me, earlier on. Shhhhh. Baby's going to hear you. Baby's going to come wailing into the world with two words: oh shit." He stood up. They looked at each other straight. She didn't know what he saw. She saw a man she had once thought she couldn't get over. She'd got over him. Only something was stopping her now from saying, simply, you don't move me.

"Mick?"

"Yes?"

"Forget the baby. It's you and me. That's all. I think we always had too many problems for you and me. Go away."

She went about her business that day, went to a dinner party that night, slept well, and didn't begin listening for the phone till the following morning. "Where the hell have you *been*?" she screamed when he finally called three days later.

Clumsily, delicately, like a couple of elephants playing a game of jackstraws, they approached each other over the next few weeks and finally one night, after they'd had a lot of drinks, she took him to bed in tipsy compassion, and he put his face against her ripe swelling flesh and asked forgiveness. "Maybe," she said, "maybe I'll forgive you," and he held onto her gently till she said, "Oh come on, Mick, I won't break, come on."

Early the next morning, hungover, sober, and filled with nameless anxiety, she gazed on the man sleeping next to her. Once she had watched him sleep and felt like Psyche gazing on Cupid. Now she noticed he was getting a bit of a double chin. She went down the hall into the deserted kitchen, made coffee and, putting a robe over her nightgown, went out onto the terrace where everything was bathed in the azure clarity of early October. The reservoir sparkled far below. The park, just beginning to turn gold, looked rich and inviting. Sitting back, lighting a cigarette, enjoying the morning view, she stared at a pigeon strutting on the ledge. She thought: "So now that you've got him back, Susannah, do you really want him?"

Chapter Twenty

In February, in the middle of a gentle thaw, their son was born.

It was a rough birth, of which Susannah retained only a few fuzzy memories. A hospital—she'd only been a patient once—to have her appendix out as a child . . . a bright corner room with green walls and prissy flowered curtains framing a spectacular river view. Mike's hand crushed in hers, every few minutes her nails digging into the palm.

"Why is it taking so long?" Mike Browne asked the doctor.

"Some do," the doctor said. "First births are often difficult."

"Can't you do something?"

"We've given her something. We can't give her too much."

"When will she go up?"

"When the pains come regularly."

"Do you want to go away, Mick?" Susannah asked the father-to-be.

"You bet. I'd love to go away and get smashed, but I won't."

"If it's a girl?"

"All right, you win. Rachel if it's a girl. And if it's a boy?"

"All right, you win. Michael, Jr., if it's a boy." Weeks of scrapping over names were ended.

"I think it's going to be an elephant," she said, bearing down on his hand.

Then she remembered a room with white tiles, bright lights, and a masked nurse saying, "Bear down now, dear, you have to push, dear: *push.*" Then sweet engulfing blackness. Twenty-four hours later, back in the green room again, filled with flowers, Mike sat beside her bed and gave her a box in which was a diamond ring the shape of a snake with ruby eyes. The card read: "From the snake you've wound around your little finger."

Then she was home, in her own bedroom done just like the green guest room at Cherryhill, pale springtime wallpaper with white linen curtains framing her view—the one she loved the best—of Central Park. She was sitting up in morning light in a big canopy bed, holding her son who looked so much like both of them with dark hair and angry brows that for the first time they said to each other: is it possible we look alike? Is it possible we *are* alike? Will this baby, blend of both of us, make us see that? Nursing the baby, ("So unnecessary and unsanitary," her sister-in-law Puss said.) she thought, how weird to have Mike Browne's son clinging there, and to have Mike himself slopped in the big chair, the morning papers at his feet, watching and grinning, teasing, making the obvious remark: "Hey Junior, that's my place." And then he had the nerve to recall another set of Sunday papers, to remember her lying naked on those papers, to remember aloud the moment of the child's conception. As if he'd clean forgotten what she could not forget: the time in between.

Still, as far as she knew, she had forgiven her erring husband. Provided he toed the line, that is. "You are on permanent probation," she said to him. And heaven help him should he take the warning lightly.

Chapter Twenty-one

About nine months after Rick was born, a portrait of Susannah Browne with her son appeared on the cover of *Life*. An incredible sunlit view of a laughing mother, with smooth strong brown arms, holding a child to the sky. It was a beautiful picture, taken by Susannah's old friend Kate Bellow, who in the past decade had become one of the magazine's star photographers. Susannah was startled and excited and pleased, first to hear that her picture would be included in a portfolio of Kate's work, then that it might be on the cover of *Life*. When she saw it, she was overwhelmed, not so much by the sight of herself in the most conspicuous spot in America as by the sheer beauty of the dark young woman and her gleaming child.

On the other hand, Mike was furious, for a variety of reasons, only some of which he admitted or realized. First there was the threat of kidnapping. "I'm surprised at Kate," he said. Kate was the only one of Susannah's friends from before her marriage that Mike had accepted, perhaps because when you dug down you discovered that Katherine Gage Bellow had been to the right schools, danced at the right parties, spent summers in Southampton before she broke away from her roots and made an independent name for herself. "Kate, at least, should have known better." Then there was the cheapness of it. "Twenty cents," he said, "that's about what you're worth." Then there was the fact that her shirt was open too far and that she had already been that year in *House and Garden* and *Vogue* and his mother was having fits over so much publicity. Finally, with an ornery look on his face, he asked: "What do they mean, 'Young Mothers of America: the Art of Kate Bellow.' *Young!* Jesus, you're ten years older than anyone else in this spread." And it was true. None of those others, the society mothers, or the celebrity mothers, or the earnest, anonymous, suburban mothers, or the urban mothers working part time at glamour jobs, or the country mothers getting back to nature could have been more than twenty-four or five. And yet not one had the vitality and glow of Susannah Browne. "I guess with me the camera lies," she said to her husband.

One thing Mike didn't mention was the caption inside, which included the interesting information that vibrant, lovely Mrs. Michael Browne, wife of Wall Street's latest wonder boy, was the former Susannah Rosoff, Barnard graduate, summa cum laude, who before her marriage had written under the name of Susan Rose. At first this annoyed, and finally amused Susannah. For six years her religion had not been mentioned, except occasionally as an uneasy joke between herself and Mike. Everyone avoided it, even Violet, as something embarrassing, uncomfortable, something it was better to ignore since most people were kind enough to ignore it, except for one or two last-stand clubs and a handful of last-stand society bigots, both old and young. Now Susannah was getting tired of turning her back on her origins, perhaps because of her son, perhaps because of some acquired confidence. Lately she had been bolder about mentions and confrontations, as if she'd decided her heritage was something to be proud of. So she challenged Mike: "Are you sure it isn't because of that caption, and *only* because of that caption, you're so mad?"

"Nonsense," he said angrily. But it silenced him.

Within a week of the picture's appearance, Susannah began receiving mail, some fifty letters all told: mash notes; crank notes from orthodox fanatics concerning her having married out of her faith; obscene proposals; billet-doux from forgotten high school and college classmates; requests for money, many of those; two offers from publishers to put her under contract to write her life story.

And then there was a strange and lengthy letter, the return address a Southern California nursing home, from one Samuel Rosoff who claimed to be her father.

There could conceivably be other Susannah Rosoffs, the man wrote, though it wasn't a usual name, but not one who looked so exactly like his own dear wife as a young mother. A meandering thirty-year history followed (the handwriting shaky, totally illegible in places), a recounting of bad luck, the desire to disappear and be thought dead, an enumeration of jobs up and down the West Coast, a chronicling of eventual peace with a good woman, too brief, interrupted by a terminal illness. "Should you wish to forgive a dying man, old beyond his years," the letter concluded, "you could write to the above address. I do not hope for you to come. If I hear nothing," the man ended, "I will understand."

"Obviously a crank," Mike Browne said at first. "Don't answer it."

"I wouldn't dream of answering it," Susannah said.

Mike looked at her sharply and said nothing. Her face had frozen in a harsh way even he had never seen. Then: "That's a relief," he said, "because you'd be just crazy enough to go out there and see, on the off chance . . ."

"It's not an off chance. That could be my father. I've always had a feeling he was alive somewhere. He could have recognized me."

"I don't understand. If you think that . . . what should we do?"

"Do? Nothing." No expression in her voice. "Forget it."

He gave her another funny look.

"It's too late," she said. "Many years too late. He deserted me and my mother. He wanted to be dead to us. Let him stay dead then, and not now try to make up to his rich daughter whose picture is in *Life* magazine."

"You're hard, Susannah." He continued to stare at her.

"I've had a good teacher," she said. She saw he didn't understand a woman's capacity for hate, any more than her capacity for love.

Samuel Rosoff was never mentioned again and was soon forgotten in the uproar of a couple of crises much closer to home. First, in December of that same fall, just before Christmas, Susannah had a second miscarriage, brought on by the death of her Uncle Dan. Her doctor warned her. "You'll have to sit still if you want to hold on to another baby. You'll have to resign yourself to becoming a vegetable for nine months." That, Susannah said, for the moment anyhow, was impossible.

Then, in January, shortly after New Year's, Violet Browne suffered a near fatal heart attack. Having the constitution of an ox, as her son gallantly observed, she survived, and would live, she was told, but only if she changed her way of life, slowed down, and stopped trying to run her huge estate as if she were still twenty-five.

So Susannah achieved her fondest wish and became mistress of Cherryhill without paying the extreme penalty of losing the mother-in-law she had come to love. For some months Mike hassled with his sister, Puss, who it turned out hated her childhood home even more than the thought of "that woman" (to her Susannah was still "that woman" who had shanghaied the innocent brother) residing there in Violet's place. Then, with his mother's connivance, Mike bought Puss out. Violet moved into a charming eighteenth-century farmhouse no more than ten minutes away and promised to come back regularly to tend the roses of Cherryhill. Painters, carpenters, and interior decorators were already at work modernizing the big house, in subtle ways loosening up the grand look of some of the rooms for the new occupants. In the sudden swift way the Brownes had of doing things, they unloaded their apartment and moved into Cherryhill in the fall of 1952, a few days before Susannah's thirty-fifth birthday.

In the dining room, the one room Susannah had left more or less the way it had been the first day she saw it, Mike Browne stood, in front of the giant silvery marlin, to toast his wife at their first party—a birthday and housewarming combined. He began caustically, humorously, in expected Mike Browne fashion, with a quote from Groucho Marx. "Marriage is an interminable Thanksgiving dinner," he said, "in which the dessert comes first." Somehow he worked his way up and out from under the hard-boiled quips to a curiously sentimental ending. ". . . So I want to drink to my wife," he said, raising his glass, "the mother of my son, and a lovely woman to come home to. I adore her. I'm glad she was born." Then he went around to her end of the table and kissed her in front of assembled family and friends. "I'm also proud of her," he added. Altogether more serious words than he'd ever spoken in all the years they'd been wed.

And she, who ordinarily had more serious words to deliver than he cared to hear, said only, "Thank you."

Chapter Twenty-two

For Mike and Susannah Browne, the period that followed seemed to be an expanding, buoyant time; well-lived, thoroughly enjoyed, its public aspects well and thoroughly documented in the popular press. If one couple represented the conspicuous prosperity of the 1950's, it was surely the Brownes, their base Cherryhill, their oyster the world, which they circled incessantly, Susannah in search of new, more interesting and important friends, Mike in search of business and play. But they always came back to Cherryhill to rest up, take stock, and count their trophies. As their New York apartment, dubbed Cherrymountain, had been a symbol of the first brassy postwar years, so Cherryhill, in their hands, became a center of gaiety, a silver lining to the gray fifties.

Built into the marriage, however, was one recurring problem; whether major or minor depended on whose viewpoint you shared, his or hers. About the time her husband turned thirty, the spring after her own thirty-fifth birthday, Susannah became aware that Mike Browne was by no means finished as far as other women were concerned.

"You won't change him," said Kitty, who was divorced from Red Jones and residing in Rome. In June of 1953 she was back for a fortnight's stay at Cherryhill. "You have to accept that from time to time those baby blue eyes are going to wander. He can't help himself. Mike *loves* women."

"And they love him," said his wife. "They didn't used to, only me. *Now!* Some weeks you can't move for the traffic. Women on the phone, asking him to serve on this committee, lend his name to that good cause. Women cluttering up his office, seeking financial advice. Women stopping by at Cherryhill to beg for money. Women in need of cheering up or calming down cornering him at parties. I can put up with his loving the species in general, and vice versa," she added. "It's when it gets to be one in particular."

"Just once you had something to worry about," said Kitty. "Poor old Di. Look at her now." A few months earlier, making what many people considered a fine match, Diana Weatherby had married Stanley Koenig, reputed to be brilliant, an economist working for the State Department. But to Kitty, her old schoolmate, Di, was now and forever "poor," not only because her new husband was only moderately well-to-do, but also because he was the kind of bore, Kitty said, who would put God himself to sleep. "Diana *was* a threat, but these others are just itches. Everyone gets itchy, even you, pal, for Christ's sake. That's human nature. Look at Mike's father. Everyone knew about those showgirls of his."

"The ones Mike picks aren't showgirls. They're . . . ladies . . ." Only Susannah could pronounce the word with such scorn. "I'm the chorus girl, don't you see?"

"No." Kitty genuinely didn't see.

"Have you ever been jealous?"

"I don't believe in jealousy."

"That's no answer."

"I was never jealous of Red Jones."

"What about Jean-Pierre?" asked Susannah.

A mean look darkened her friend's sunny countenance.

"Well?"

"All right. Yes."

"And?"

"I rise above it."

"I can't."

Even a passing fling on Mike's part with a certain sort of girl was to Susannah an insult and a threat.

There was Patsy Clay, for instance, wife of Charlie Clay, the table salt heir. During the winter of 1953, when Mike often found himself in Chicago (where Susannah wouldn't be caught dead), the Clays had put him up and lavishly entertained him in their Lake Forest mansion, a place where everything was the color or texture of gold. Susannah and Mike had once joked about Patsy Clay, whom they christened the "Golden Mommy." Implacably gentile, blonde, and glowing, Patsy always looked as if en route to a tennis game. She wore white, winter and summer, and gold bobby pins in her hair. Her person was groomed, her life organized, her voice fluting, her riches vast. Among her most prized possessions, along with the gilded harp and the school of Della Robbia fountain, were two blonde and glowing children about whom she talked incessantly. But after his winter visits, Mike wasn't making cracks about the Golden Mommy. "Patsy's a lot of fun," he announced, "when she lets her hair down," and insisted on inviting the Clays to Cherryhill for a spring weekend.

Susannah observed that the Golden Mommy had indeed taken her hair out of its bobbies so it could fall seductively over one eye. And fun was the least of what Mike and Patsy seemed to be having Saturday night at the Plainfield's dance. "What's happened to Lake Forest?" Susannah asked Mike. "Me," he said.

Sunday morning, awake too early, Susannah was aware of Mike's absence. At noon he was still gone, as was Patsy. Fuming, Susannah sat in a provocative new bikini by the pool, warding off passes from hungover Charlie Clay and watching her small son, who at three was already swimming without water wings. "Where's Daddy?" the boy kept asking. Finally they appeared, sweet and wholesome as the day, Mike and Patsy, coming from the direction of the great woods, in blue jeans and old sweaters, with binoculars around their necks.

"We've been on a walk," said Mike.

"Some walk," said his wife.

"I wanted to find that pileated woodpecker for Patsy."

The Golden Mommy shared Mike's passion for wildlife, an enthusiasm mysterious to Susannah who, in spite of Violet's attempts to convert her, continued to refer to bird watchers as "pecker watchers."

"Did you find it?" Susannah asked.

"No," said Patsy, blue eyes fixed on Mike, dimples piercing her cheeks as she smiled. "But we found lots of other things."

"I'll bet," Susannah said, noticing that under the loose old sweater Patsy was wearing absolutely nothing.

Sunday night when Mike returned home from driving the Clays to the airport, he found on his pillow a dead sea gull, Susannah's trophy from a walk of her own along the beach. "What's that for?" he asked. "Symbolism," she said.

Over Fourth of July, when they met up with the Clays in Newport, Susannah saw to it that there were no more long walks for Mike and Patsy, or even long stretches on the dance floor. The following fall when in Chicago on business Mike stayed with friends other than the Clays.

But then, by the following fall, Marie Laure de Brissac came into Susannah's life, arriving in New York from Paris, without her husband, for an indefinite stay. Everyone gave parties for

Marie Laure, including the Brownes, and for a while Susannah found her refreshing. But presently she noticed that Mike and Marie Laure, whenever they were together, spoke French, a language Mike had learned in early childhood and had forbidden Susannah to speak. "You speak French," he'd said unfairly to the former Susan Rose, "like Bert Lahr speaks English."

"Your 'usband," Marie Laure said to Susannah one day, for all her blue blood rolling her eyes like some cheap soubrette, "is an *homme changé* in French. A curious phenomenon, no, the way people change from language to *langue*. In French Brownie 'as an elegant wit, *très fin*, a pity you can't understand."

"Oh, I understand," Susannah said.

"You know he's a great student of Voltaire?"

"*Mike?* Fat chance."

"Oh yes, he says in the army he read all of Voltaire and Stendhal."

Susannah further observed that Mike, who called chanteuses "croakers," was suddenly keen to hear Piaf and was buying her records as well as those of Josephine Baker and Juliette Greco. One night, home from escorting Marie Laure to a benefit performance of the Comédie Française (an occasion at which Susannah, after all, would not be caught dead), he found a dozen of his favorite ties, including four vintage Charvets Marie Laure had given him, sliced in two. "What's that for?" he said angrily. "More symbolism," she said.

Soon thereafter Marie Laure went back to Paris and for awhile peace reigned in the Browne household. By the following August, when Mike and Susannah went to Deauville for the de Brissac's costume ball, Susannah was almost nostalgic for the days of Marie Laure and the Golden Mommy. By then she really had someone to worry about: Kate Bellow, a flirtation that was not such a joke, Kate being, after all, Susannah's old friend. "With Kate," Susannah said to Kitty Jones later, "I began to realize you were right. Either I'd have to 'wise' above or go mad."

The de Brissac ball—an eighteenth-century extravaganza to celebrate the two hundredth birthday of the family chateau—was the first of those great, glittering, postwar international occasions for which people flew in from all over the world, having spent months planning their costumes, wigs, jewels. Nothing was too much trouble for a gala that was sure to be written up in half a dozen languages and photographed in black and white, and color, for all the magazines and papers that counted, and talked about by everyone worth knowing for the next six months—or at least till an even more lavish party was thrown. The Brownes, however, in a superb gesture of insouciance, had arrived from Greece the morning of the party, sunburned and unkempt, trailing packages and duffel bags like gypsies, and improvised disguises that were the hit or disgrace of the party, depending on how you viewed it. He went as a pirate, with toy shop mustache, a black patch over his right eye, and one of his wife's gold loops in his left ear. As the pirate's captive, she did nothing more than wash her own hair, letting it dry unset and fly wild, and slash to ribbons, just barely within bounds of decency, her most clinging and expensive dress. Amid all the satins, velvets, laces, and plumes, the Brownes stood out like a couple of alley cats in a lawn of peacocks. The men took after her, the women after him, and the press after both of them.

Among the photographers was an acerbic Kate Bellow, covering the party for *Life*. Ordinarily above such tasks, she told Susannah, she had accepted the assignment for laughs and a record fee, but it occurred to Susannah, almost immediately, that there could be another reason for her friend's presence. "I want to talk to you," she heard Mike say to Kate, who wore work clothes, black pants, and a brilliant purple shirt, streaked hair pulled back in a ponytail. "When you get through, will you find me?"

Earlier that summer in Los Angeles, at the Beverly Hills Hotel (where Susannah wouldn't be caught dead), Mike, attending a conference, and Kate, photographing a star, had run into each other. They had spent the evening together, an occasion reported by both of them subsequently to Susannah in high hilarity and convincing detail. Looking at the pair now, Susannah wondered why she'd been so amused.

"I'll try to find you," Kate said. "Right now I want to find that creep Tony George. He's supposed to be going around with me telling me who to photograph." Susannah had never noticed before how much Kate's husky voice resembled that of Diana Weatherby.

"I'll go around with you," Mike said.

"Buzz off, Brownie, I know your tricks."

He looked after her with a silly grin on his face. "Cute girl," he said. Cute? *Kate?*

Much later, Susannah Browne, on the arm of Robert Garden—Sasha to his friends—who was beginning to be internationally known, said to Carol Plainfield, "Have you seen Mike?" Even disguised as a powdered Gainsborough duchess, Carol still wore her impenetrable sapphire spectacles.

"No. Have you seen God's gift, Pete Plainfield?"

"Earlier. Not for awhile."

"*I* know . . ." It was hard to find a couple of stray husbands at a party of five hundred that stretched out over several acres of landscaped grounds, but Carol had a trained nose and tracked them down in a luminous pavilion by the lake, where the sweetest of three orchestras played. At the edge of the dance floor, half a dozen happy, laughing, transfixed men stood around a single woman, a hoydenish Hogarth Shrimp Girl. It was Tootie Blake, the new sexpot comedienne who had taken Broadway by storm the previous season. "Do you *believe* those men?" Carol said. "I thought Pete had fallen on his ass with that one." Peter Plainfield had begun to back shows, fancied himself a connoisseur of flesh, a spotter of talent, and had been the major investor in Tootie's smash hit. "She *can't* sing, she *can't* dance, and what she *can* do she's not allowed to show on the stage," Carol continued. "Still, she has every man in the audience panting and the women hooked, wondering how she does it."

But the Tootie Blakes of this world weren't Mike's problem. He wasn't with the gang. He was with Kate Bellow whose cameras were abandoned, whose neat hair was shaken loose. (What was it about him that made neat girls shake loose?) They were dancing the newest way, the way the French kids danced, arms wrapped around each other's necks, barely moving, to a melancholy song about dead leaves. "This is a drag," Susannah said to Robert Garden. "Let's go back to the good music."

At the chateau, in a mirrored room set up like a night club, where an all-girl mambo band played frenetically, Susannah Browne proceeded to put on a show with the host—Robert Garden didn't dance—such as she had not given since the last winter she was Susan Rose, dating Bill Wolfe. Afterward Mike said it was a whore's performance, skirts up to her navel, breasts flung around like basketballs. But he exaggerated. She was sexy indeed, and quite outrageous, but always in control, allure expressed in the flick of a wrist, the shake of an arm, the precise swivel of hips, in a wink, a moistening of lips, a snapping of fingers, a perfect sense of rhythm. Whatever she and the host were doing, it was sufficiently intriguing for other people to stop dancing and form a circle around them. The gelid-faced players, with their butch haircuts and tuxedos, began watching the dancers and synchronizing music to movements. Showing off, Susannah was happy in herself and Mike Browne was far from her thoughts.

Then she caught sight of her husband's angry face among

the ring of onlookers, saw him motioning her to come on, as if she was the one in the wrong. Shortly thereafter he was beside her. "Show's over," he said, and with an iron grip ushered her off the floor.

"You're drunk," he accused, in the curtained, quilted privacy of their suite in Deauville's grandest old hotel.

"*I* don't get drunk."

"You didn't used to when I first knew you."

"I was having a good time."

"You were making a fool of yourself."

"*I* was? What do you think you were doing, wrapped around Kate Bellow. Couldn't you at least keep your hands off *my* friends?"

"I believe you are pathological. She's a smart girl. I like her. Period."

"Have you got into her smart pants yet?"

"You're so vulgar."

"You know the root of vulgar? Vulgaris, Latin, meaning of the common people. I *am* of the common people and I don't buy your upper-class ways. I believe in the marriage vows."

"So do I. Love, honor, cherish. Because you cherish someone doesn't mean you stop connecting with all other people of the opposite sex."

"I should give you a taste of your own medicine. *I* should decide to connect with someone of the opposite sex. Sasha Garden, for instance, who has been after me for a while." She wished Mike could see his own face. "But of course you'd say: men and women are different."

"I wouldn't say anything of the kind. I'd say I wouldn't care. Maybe that's your problem, Slick. After eight years of marriage to me what you need is a fling with someone else. Not Sasha Garden, of course."

"Hah!"

"And I wouldn't want to hear every detail. But it's no big deal. Unless you let your emotions get involved."

"Bullshit. I'll tell you. For me it would be a big deal. I've had flings, plenty of them, long before I ever met you. I don't believe in that kind of junk. Not when you have what we have. If I had an affair with someone it would be extremely serious. *Love*. And then I'd leave you for him. That's the truth."

He shook his head and smiled. She was so earnest sometimes, so grave, when life wasn't always meant to be grave. But he found her earnestness appealing.

"You shouldn't get so upset," he said. "It's not good for your blood pressure."

"Go away."

"You don't think Kate Bellow means anything. Do you? Come on . . ."

"Oh, to hell with it, Brownie," Susannah said. Calling him that—not Mike or Mick, but Brownie—meant something, she wasn't sure what. "I'm learning."

That night he made love to her as if she were precious. That night she received his love as if it were something less than precious, something possibly expendable, or interchangeable.

Perhaps they were both better off for the adjustment. In any case, Kate Bellow soon drifted out of their lives, discovering, as would-be interlopers of both sexes kept discovering, that neither Browne could or would, apparently, do for long without the other. After the routing of Kate, things at Cherryhill seemed to reach a sort of equilibrium again. Because Rick was no longer a baby to be left with nurses, but a little person both of his parents enjoyed, there were, beginning the winter he turned four, many sweet, funny, unplanned days that centered around the boy. There were trips for just the three of them, when Mike and Susannah would take the child off to a quiet beach or up to the Adirondacks. Though it wasn't a second honeymoon, exactly, still it seemed to all who knew them that the Brownes finally had a marriage and were a family. If there was a shadow on those years, people who knew the

Brownes said it wasn't Mike's silly wandering eye, but Susannah's apparent inability to hold onto a second baby.

For other members of the Squad these were good years also, marked by cheerful events: marriages (Red Jones to Georgie de Groot, the accordion playing playgirl who was steady as a rock and loved Red); Mimi Bryan, number-one bachelor girl of New York to her long-standing beau, John Packard, in a last-ditch maneuver (after he'd engaged himself to someone else); spectacular romances; the continuing international running around of Kitty Jones; the birth of babies (notably triplets to Georgie and Red); much prosperity, many good times.

With two terrible exceptions: the deaths of Jay Lawrence and Peter Plainfield.

Unlike some of the other violent happenings among the group, Jay's suicide in the autumn of 1953 went largely unnoticed because Jay, living in Bermuda, his liver rotting, more and more a recluse, had dropped so far out of sight people barely remembered him. Only a few old friends, mostly women like Mimi Packard and Susannah Browne, kept up with him. Only a few people attended Jay's funeral. Only a few people knew the details of his death: that having been warned by his doctor never to take another drink, Jay went off the wagon one morning and a few days later shot himself.

"Why?" Kitty said to Susannah the following summer in Rome when the Brownes came for a visit. "Why did he want to kill himself drinking?" Susannah said, as if it was an explanation: "Once he asked me if I'd ever been jilted. I said, 'yes, once.' He said, 'I've been jilted many times and with my sort of life will be jilted many times again.' "

On the other hand, the Plainfield case was one of the less private, more sensational tragedies in the annals of the very rich.

Peter Plainfield, friend from childhood of Red Jones and

Mike Browne, copper heir, playboy, all-round good sport, had become, in the last few years one of the most successful Broadway producers. In the spring of 1955 his show, *Playgirl,* starring Tootie Blake, was going into its third year to standing-room-only crowds. He was also something of a ladies' man. One June night his beautiful and notoriously jealous wife, Carol, had accidentally shot him dead, mistaking him for a burglar. But many people, including the state of New York, had questioned just how accidental the shooting had been. The press had had a field day. There were nine hundred mourners at the funeral, while in the street, roped off by the police, stood an estimated two thousand curiosity seekers. The flags of the slain man's clubs had flown at half-mast, because Pete was also a man's man. Nobody in or around New York, in or out of the Squad, talked of anything else for months. Even after Carol Plainfield had been cleared by the grand jury, the talk and news stories continued, as much as for *Playgirl* as for poor old Pete and poor old Carol. "If it hadn't been for that godamned show," Mike said, "they could have kept the godamned thing out of the papers."

"Do you realize that's four gone?" Mike Browne said one night shortly after Pete's death, while studying the picture of Kitty St. John's wedding party, which hung on his dressing room wall. "It makes you wonder, who next?"

"Five," Susannah corrected, already tucked in. "You've forgotten Jay Lawrence. But let's not talk about it." Reality was linen sheets and soft blankets, a silk coverlet, not death.

"Well, now," said Mike the gambler, "five out of fourteen in eight years. Interesting odds. At that rate, ten out of fourteen in sixteen years . . . it's riskier to have been a member of Kit's wedding than president of a banana republic."

"I *don't* want to talk about it."

"That's not like you, not having something smartass to say," getting into bed beside her, seeming to get larger, more like a big dog every year, though in fact his weight had not gone up more than five pounds since she married him.

"It gives me the creeps," she said, "so shut up. Sooner or later a hundred out of a hundred die. Here's to the next forty years," switching off the light, putting her arms around him.

In fact they had left to them eighteen months, three weeks, and approximately forty hours.

Part III

Chapter Twenty-three

The night she killed him was the longest night of the year and they were on their way home from a Christmas party.

Had their host been anyone other than who he was, Susannah and Mike wouldn't have gone. Nothing else going on that night could have tempted them out into the bitter frozen darkness, she with a cold, he with a bad back; not Puss and George's caroling, always a beautiful affair and a Long Island tradition, to which they'd gone every year since their marriage; not Elena Worden's annual cocktail buffet, sure to include amusing new people; not Grace Baxter's debut, forecast as the extravaganza of the decade; not even the small dinner at the dowager Mrs. Cuttredge's (who'd once barred Susannah from her house, kept Susannah out of clubs) for the world's leading soprano. The Brownes were hard to get these days, especially now that Mike was a name of sorts. Even if they accepted an invitation, chances were, friends remarked sourly, they'd back out at the last minute. But even for those two, an invitation to the Sutton Place house of Robert Garden was a command.

Robert Alexander Garden—Sasha—ultra-rich, ultra-powerful, origins vaguely Roumanian, was the sort of man, Kitty Jones once told Susannah, who spent a million dollars a year staying *out* of the papers. Secrecy, she said, was his vice, a pleasure second only to influencing the economic and foreign policies of governments around the world. Women, she added caustically, for all the man's reputation, were far down the list.

Mike and Susannah had first spent real time with Sasha a few weeks after the de Brissac ball, in Monte Carlo where Susannah's losses at roulette were more than wiped out by Mike's winnings at the baccarat tables.

"That," Susannah had said to Kitty one night at the Casino, watching Sasha at play, "is the worst looking man in the world. I've never paid enough attention to him before to notice."

"That," said Kitty, "is what I used to think. He has to concentrate on you," herself gazing speculatively at the swarthy, pockmarked face and burly body of Sasha Garden.

"Hey!" Susannah said, looking at Kitty, looking at Sasha, "I've had a thought . . ." His dark eyes, she had to admit, were hypnotic when he focused on you.

"Never!"

"I don't know . . ." Kitty's replacement for the polo player Clark "Larky" Harrison was a suave Moroccan prince, a disaster as far as Susannah was concerned. Sasha Garden, divorced for many years from the mother of his only daughter, was said to be looking for a wife. "You seem to go for Calibans."

"Sasha's too remote and serious for me," Kitty said. "Not enough nights off with that one."

Subsequently, Sasha Garden had become close to the Brownes. Mike had done him a favor. He, in turn, had done Mike a bigger favor, and one day, Mike Browne, unlike Sasha not averse to public notice, found himself, in connection with a major financial coup, on the front page of the *New York Times.* Sasha Garden was important to Mike and to Susannah. He was the first man since her marriage she had felt a kinship with. He had ferreted out her early articles and grilled her about the writing she had long ago given up. The two of them, Sasha said, were a pair of elegant outsiders.

Susannah never speculated on how much their friendship mattered to her; instead she talked constantly about matching him up with her drifting friend, Kitty.

But even if she hadn't been fond of him, in who else's house might she have met, in the past year, the president of the United States, the prime minister of England, the *grand eminence* of France, *and* Marlene Dietrich.

Nonetheless, she had gone that night under duress.

She had fought with Mike before they'd ever left for their fatal evening. The next day she'd been smart enough to admit that to her lawyer and the police. Rick's nurse would have told them if Susannah hadn't: of the loud angry voices when she knocked on the bedroom door to bring the little boy, after his supper, to see his parents. Nanny Fergus, about to be fired, no fan of Susannah's, would have related that when she'd opened the door the attitudes of Mr. and Mrs. Browne had scarcely been peaceful. They'd been having words all right, Susannah told the cops. He'd waved the red flag and she'd reacted. But that was part of their marriage, dear God, part of the legend and reputation of the mercurial, excitable Brownes, she kept saying. It didn't mean anything. So she told her story.

"Let's finesse it," Susannah said. Mike had come home early from his office, complaining that his back was killing him—an old ski injury acting up—and was lying on the bed hunched up, trying to find a comfortable position, reading a report. "It's so bloody cold," she said, put down the whiskey and lemon she'd been drinking, and rubbed his back. "The papers say it's going down to zero. The roads are terrible. I'll call and say we're both sick." She provided a series of sneezes for authenticity.

"Not possible. You don't do that to Robert Garden. But cheer up. You know who's going to be there?" He dropped a rare political name, a name to thrill a people collector like Susannah.

"How do you know?"

"Natalie told me." Pause. "Now don't look like that."

"God*damn,* Mike . . ." Natalie Jones. Red Jones's tomboy baby sister, grown up silken and smooth and old beyond her years. At fourteen she'd been taken for a debutante, at sixteen for a twenty-year-old actress. Now, at nineteen, she was *the* new great international girl, always around the Gardens because Christa Garden, another great girl, was Natalie's best friend. New York was a city of great new girls these days, girls with dandelion hair and smudged eyes and pale mouths, and whatever the first name, the last name was Youth.

"Where did you see Natalie? I thought you'd cut that out."

"Where do you think I saw her? In your favorite shop."

Natalie Jones—prettiest debutante to come off the assembly line since her former sister-in-law, Kitty St. John, and in no way college material—was currently putting in a stint at a Fifth Avenue jewelry store. "I adore spending eight hours a day with diamonds," she said.

"I see. Did you take her to lunch?" Stiffening, accusing. Yes, Susannah Browne admitted frankly to the police, ever since the previous winter when Natalie had come crashing into their lives at a party given by Red and Georgie Jones, she had been concerned about the way Natalie had been throwing herself at Mike.

"As a matter of fact, I did. Want to make something of it?"

"You *bet!* Is she going to be there tonight?"

"She's a fixture at Garden's. If that girl stayed out of trouble and played her cards well, she might marry above herself . . ." looking at his wife who'd done, in his eyes anyhow, just that. "But whoever listened to me?"

"Did you, Mike? Did you give her advice? That's your specialty, isn't it? You can go by yourself tonight." Voice rising.

"You're not going to start the Natalie bit again?"

"Damn right I am. I can't stand to see you make a fool of yourself one more time." Sneezing, reaching for a Kleenex, she knocked over her whiskey glass.

"Cut the act, Susannah. Go take your bath. We don't want to be late."

"It's not an act," she said very loudly, before another fit of sneezing overtook her. *"I've had it with you."*

That was the moment Nanny and Rick entered and Susannah, instantly transformed, took her dark and elfin son, nearly six, who was clutching a stuffed dinosaur, onto the bed and nuzzled him because he was her pet, her cub, and she doted on him and began a conversation with him concerning the eating habits of the brontosaur.

"Bath," Mike said.

"He wants me to get pneumonia," she said to her son, but moved as her husband ordered.

Once in the tub, having frothed up the bubbles, she called the child in. He was probably getting too old for that, chatting with his mother while she bathed, but she had never gone by the book. The little boy came in and they talked their usual water talk, about bubbles and iridescence, and what makes some soaps float, about fishes and gills and why people can't breathe under water. As she chatted, lying back in deep pine scented water, she washed herself with a big yellow soap, cleaning, pumicing and perfecting the no longer perfect body of Susannah Browne, though in the tub she retained an illusion of perfection: plump bosom, swathed with bubbles, high before her; shapely arms and smooth knees, ripe and glistening in oiled water.

The little boy stood there grinning, admiring, firing questions at her, when suddenly behind him stood his father, also grinning, seeming to admire. But then his father did something odd. He took an ashtray piled with butts from the table beside her lounging chair (that kind of bathroom; furnished; big as most bedrooms; verdant with plants) and dumped the contents into the perfumed bath water.

It was a mess not only remembered by the child, but also duly noted by Nanny and maid and commented on. Her son stared, not knowing whether to laugh or cry, then ran from the room. As she cursed, Mike said nothing, simply stood there, and when she'd got out of the tub and cleaned the mess off herself, she lashed out at him, trying to scratch his face with her long red nails, but he held her slippery wrists fast, his fingers like handcuffs. He was very strong.

"What's all that about?" she said. "To remind me to empty the ashtrays?"

"There are servants to empty the ashtrays. That's to remind you who's boss around here, who pays the bills, who runs the show, and who's taken damn good care of you over the years, Miss Rose. That's all."

Rick had now returned, in his hands another full ashtray, this one from the bedroom. "Me, too," he shrieked, heading toward the tub.

"No," Mike said, taking his hands, removing the ashtray, gently. "This is between your mother and me. Go on, sport, scram. I ever catch you being fresh to your mother I'll whale the daylights out of you," the last words, as she recollected, the father ever said to his son.

Her combat dress was black: a wide-skirted brocade evening suit, black lace stockings, black satin pumps with big paste buckles. There were diamonds in her ears and at her wrists, and at her throat a diamond and topaz clip holding in place a twist of apricot chiffon. She decided she looked elegant, in a ripe way, in spite of her cold. Thirty-nine wasn't old: wasn't even middle-aged.

"O.K.?" she said, showing herself to Mike, who waited in the front hall.

"I didn't know it was Halloween," he said. "I thought it was Christmastime."

That was his way, love by insult. Lots of women found it attractive. So had she, long ago. There was something else for a maid to report: "Madam went out the front door mad, I can tell you. But she was always going out mad."

She insisted on driving. He had to be in some pain to agree, not enjoying the sensation of being her passenger. They took her car, a sports car she had never mastered the handling of. Switching on the radio, responding to the purr of the motor, sniffing the leather, she felt a familiar stimulation and enchantment, and observed her pleasure with a certain cynicism.

Usually she talked continually as she drove. But except for the radio announcer, no voices would have been heard in the sleek car that night. Not till they were turning off the East River Drive, a minute away from their destination, did he break the silence: "I don't really think you look like a witch."

"It never occurred to me you thought I looked like a witch. I thought you meant the colors, black and orange."

"Your problem is you have no sense of humor."

"I don't like you." She drew up behind a taxi in front of Garden's house, a blaze of lights, where an attendant stood ready to garage the car.

Mike smiled. "You look nice, Susannah."

Out of the taxi stepped Natalie Jones.

"I mean I *really* don't like you," Susannah said, tasting the words like a new and delightful dish, words certainly heard by Garden's uniformed man who opened the door.

"That's too bad," Mike said, "since you're stuck with me."

In the gutter, Natalie Jones dropped the entire contents of her purse. "Can I help," said Mike Browne, as his wife hurried into the house. "Let me help, Nat . . ."

Chapter Twenty-four

Dinner at Robert Garden's was like dining in a very badly designed museum, Susannah, the museum expert, always said.

Crowding the walls everywhere were the finest examples of impressionists and fauves outside of the Orangerie in Paris, clumsily framed in heavy gold, and hung so closely that they canceled each other out. Filling the rooms were priceless French and English antiques, handsome and brittle as the women who moved among them. Cluttering every available surface were astonishing objects, some grand, some amusing, all with histories, what Susannah called Napoleon's shaving mug, Marie Antoinette's hairbrush, Alexander Hamilton's dueling pistols, and Henry the Eighth's toothpick. Chandeliers flashed, parquet floors gleamed, boiserie glowed, carpets sank under your evening slippers like moss, velvet curtains held back the cruel night, yet the overwhelming feeling of the place was cold, as if it were never inhabited long enough to take the chill off it.

"It's *too much,* Sasha," she said, studying six new paintings that had invaded what had been one of the few empty bits of wall in the public rooms of the house. "It's not restful."

"Write me a memo," he teased. A specially designed tuxedo did wonders for his stocky body. "Better yet, talk to the girls."

"Which girls?"

"Christa and Natalie. I'm dumping the whole problem of the house in their laps."

"Rat," she said.

In the candle-lit dining room, set up imperial café style with round tables for eight and festooned with holly, tinsel, flocks of silvery angels (the girls' handiwork, no doubt), Susannah found her seat at the host's table. She was between the world-famous guest of honor and a difficult but distinguished octogenarian poet, a flattering place but the sort Susannah had come to expect as the city's most talented conversationalist. Her specialty was making the elderly feel naughtily young and the famous feel wickedly anonymous. Mike, she noted, two tables away, was also at an accustomed spot, between the less than dazzling wife of the guest of honor and Natalie Jones. His specialty was to make a dowdy woman feel beautiful; his reward, a genuine beauty on his other side.

Throat sore, eyes heavy, emotions uneasy, Susannah had to work harder than usual, talked less amusingly than she might about the unseasonable weather, the cold in her head, and was grateful when the host came to her rescue by involving the entire table in a conversation centered, naturally, on himself. She was even more grateful when during dessert, while the elderly poet had excused himself, Garden left the fashionable young woman on his right (her husband, a freshman senator, was already being talked of as presidential material) and came for a moment to sit beside Susannah and ordered her home. "You're a mess," he said, not unkindly. "Why did you come, to give us all the flu?"

"I didn't want to come," she said, "but try to keep Mike away from a chance to see that one," looking balefully in the direction of her husband who had apparently done his duty and was now collecting his reward, flirting with the lovely Natalie, a vision in champagne chiffon, her arms and neck gleaming like milk glass in the candlelight. Her only jewelry was a pair of long sparkling earrings; one of them kept coming off, and he helped her screw it back on.

"There are no flies on Mike," Sasha's smile when he made a bad joke resembled the Cheshire cat. "Only a Nat, so to speak. She *is* exquisite, but I find her difficult to talk to," camera eyes focusing, dilating, contracting. "Do me a favor, pet," he added, "as soon as dinner's over, disentangle that husband of yours and go home. Gesundheit!"

But before she could go to him, he had come to her, an unheard-of occurrence. "I want to go home, Susannah," he said. He seemed rather drunk from trying to dull the pain of his back.

At the door Susannah fished in her purse for the car keys.

"*You're* not driving," said their host, seeing them out.

"Better me than Mike."

"Let me send you home in my car. I'll have someone drive yours out tomorrow."

"Thanks, no," said Mike.

"Be careful," Garden called after them. "It's going to be a skating rink out there."

Afterward, Susannah's version was that they'd been as silent on the way home as on the way in. He had perhaps made some remarks about her driving and the fact that she never should have bought a sports car. She had perhaps told him to shut up. He had perhaps put his life into the hands of the Lord and closing his eyes, dozed.

When they reached the entrance of Cherryhill, she stopped the car. He got out to open the heavy, iron gate. No more gatekeeper to honk for: the last gatekeeper long since had gone. Now the gatehouse was fixed up and rented for a princely sum to friends. This winter, it so happened, to Mimi and John Packard who were building a house a few miles to the north of Cherryhill.

Mike unlocked the chain, pushed first one gate and then the other and stood back against the elegant wrought iron, his face ironic in the yellow headlights, motioning her to come on. She shifted into reverse instead of first, then found first. Impatiently he motioned again, the look of condescension growing. She loathed him for his impatience. As she gunned the car through the gate she hit a patch of ice, spun, slammed on the brake. The car came to a stop in a ditch, against a tree.

"Mick, Mick," she screamed to the man lying beside the gate. "*Stupid!* Why didn't you get out of the way? I love you, can you hear me? I love you."

For the first time since the day she'd met him, Mike did not answer back.

John and Mimi Packard found her senseless in the frozen gravel beside her husband's body.

Driving to the hospital, next to his blanket-wrapped body stretched out in the Packard's station wagon, she could say nothing.

"Did the car go out of control?" John Packard asked.

She nodded.

"He's still alive. I can feel a pulse."

But by the time they reached the hospital, his heart had stopped beating. "It's not possible," she said.

"I'm afraid it is," said Packard.

"My *baby,*" she sobbed hysterically. "My poor baby."

"He's very young," Packard said. "In some ways that's easier."

"I don't mean my son. I mean *Mike.*" Then she said: "Will you handle this? No one else?" Then she said, "Get in touch with Robert Garden." Afterward she became incoherent and they put her in a room and held her forcibly until her own doctor came and knocked her out with a sedative.

She remembered nothing of this, nor of the next morning when John Packard came back to question her, nor of the next afternoon when the police came. The doctor would not let her return to the scene of the accident for several days. By then it was completely blanketed by a fall of snow. He allowed her to go, deeply sedated, to the funeral and the entire family was protected from reporters.

Chapter Twenty-five

Long afterward, people of a certain group talked about the astonishing way the Browne case was hushed up and played down so that there was no official suggestion whatsoever of foul play, of the death being anything but a grisly accident. Still fresh in everybody's mind, of course, was the circus that had surrounded the Plainfield case two years earlier.

And here, only a couple of years later, was Susannah Browne, braking the wrong way on a skid—her story, anyhow—killing her attractive, prominent husband; a manslaughterer, involved in an accident only slightly less ambiguous than the Plainfield shooting and receiving a mere murmur in the press. Back page news items in the *Times* and *Tribune*, headlining the brief story, "Financier-sportsman killed in road accident," plus extensive and dignified obituaries. A day's flurry in the tabloids: the death of the "prominent millionaire sportsman" labeled a "holiday tragedy." There was a wire service story picked up by a dozen big city out-of-town papers in parts of the country where the Browne family was known. There was nothing in *Newsweek*. There was a "Milestone" in *Time*, but no story, no flip socio-historic observation of the tragedy in the national affairs section, the sort the magazine (which had done a job on the Plainfields) delighted in.

More to the point, there was no inquest and no investigation by a grand jury.

Timing was said to be one bit of luck. Christmas was not a favorite week to dig and hound on the part of the New York press. The greatest digger of them all, who recognized no seasons, the scurrilous and indefatigable Tony George, had been, some months earlier, fired from his job for having cost the paper one libel suit too many. Tony might have given Susannah a bad time, but he'd been run out of town, quite literally, by two prominent husbands who swore that if he ever showed his face again in any of their haunts they would shoot him. Nor was this the time of year in which the Long Island State Police were at their most alert. There had already been so many automobile fatalities during that holiday week that police later called it "Black Christmas." The police were weary. It was easy to lump Mike Browne's death into the whole grim seasonal package.

Mainly, the tone of the affair had been set by John Packard, who had said to Susannah the night of the accident, "No, no, you couldn't have mixed the foot pedals up. Obviously the car skidded when you braked. The road was ice. *You* didn't kill him. The *car* killed him. Remember that, Susannah. Your mind gets all mixed up at times like this."

John Packard had gone with the police and the police photographer and one or two reporters the next day and reenacted the accident. He was, after all, not only a lawyer but, he and his wife were also the sole witnesses. Already a fresh fall of snow had obscured the tire marks. He talked to the detectives who questioned the Browne household and the ones who had interviewed certain members of Robert Garden's staff, certain guests at the party, and Garden himself. He had described the quality of the Brownes' relationship. "Fighting was their bread and wine," he said. "They were getting on better than they ever had in their lives."

Then, from the offices of Robert Alexander Garden a few well-placed calls had been made to help quiet things down in one way and help speed things up in another.

On the morning of December 24, the Nassau County chief of police issued a statement pronouncing the death an accident and the case closed.

Early in the afternoon of the same day—Christmas Eve day —a service was held, not in New York, not even in the village church at the foot of Cherryhill, but at the graveside, attended only by the grieving immediate family: his mother, his uncles and aunts, his sister and brother-in-law, his widow, and his small son who held onto his mother with one hand, in his other held a red and white football pennant, souvenir of the game, Rick's first, his father had taken him to the previous month.

On the coffin was a blanket, not of chrysanthemums, as would have been likely this time of year, but of roses, red American Beauties. The card was very peculiar, considering the circumstances. It read, in Susannah's own handwriting: "To Mick Browne from Susan Rose: you never know till you've lost it."

Had everyone not been so grief-stricken, there might have been a few raised eyebrows over that one.

Only one prominent Hearst man, a purple prosist whose specialties were crime and social history, smelled a story. He was also a sports car buff who believed that Susannah's particular vehicle, to do what it had done, could not have skidded; would have had to be driven, and driven hard.

A week or so after the beginning of the year, he began poking around, asking people questions, digging back into the past, into the courtship of Mike Browne and Susan Rose, and the early days of their marriage. He did other research, too, preparing a long feature on ill-starred Cinderellas. But the star of the piece would be the one who had been let alone: Susannah Browne. Susannah got a phone call, warning her that a troublemaker was on her tail. Driven by some primitive instinct of self-preservation, sensing that this man was not the sort to be pressured off a piece of investigative reporting by Sasha Garden's hired thugs, she acted as she had once or twice in the past: she asked Violet Browne for help.

For the first weeks after Mike's death, Violet had kept Rick with her in the eighteenth-century farmhouse. Now, at the moment the famous reporter began poking around in the Brownes' affairs, Rick was home again with his mother, who focused her entire attention on the child. He was her anchor, her reason to live. She drank nothing but a little wine with meals, no more of the hard stuff that had been creeping up on her in recent years so that people began to notice a thickening, a film over her sharp personality, like the beginnings of a haze that might lift, but also might settle into heavy fog.

Other members of the family wondered why Violet had delivered the little boy up to the possibly hysterical, possibly dangerous woman so soon. "Because they needed each other," Violet said. "Because the doctors advised it."

By his grandmother Rick had been told simply that his father had died in a motor accident and that he was in heaven. "I don't know if you will want to correct that," Violet, the High Episcopalian, had said to Susannah the day she brought the boy back. Susannah, aged a dozen years in a month, had given her mother-in-law a strange smile and a strange answer: "I wouldn't dream of correcting it," she said. "He's too young to understand about purgatory."

That afternoon, in the library of Cherryhill, in front of a

blazing fire, the gleam of silver tea things between them, the women had talked idly. Violet skimmed the surface of the days Rick had been with her, talking about the books they'd read, the games he'd played, the food he'd eaten, complimenting Susannah on his pretty manners, his curiosity, his good temper. Only when Violet, taking her leave, stood by the front door of the house that had once been hers, that now belonged to the woman who had caused the death of her son, only then did she say to her daughter-in-law, her former protégé and pet: "For the sake of the boy, Susannah, we must believe it was an accident, a horrible tragic accident."

Then Susannah tried to speak, and Violet, who would die before she lost control, held up her hand. "Don't say anything, my dear. Sometimes there are no words."

"Once he told me that," Susannah said, turning away from the blue gaze, so like his, understanding that from Violet there would be no absolution. But then she turned back: "He used those very words when we reconciled, before Rick was born." And it was Violet's turn to look away from the green gaze, knowing that Susannah would always remember: once, you and I conspired.

After that, every few days Violet would stop by to see Rick and chat with Susannah concerning domestic matters and problems of the estate, advising her not to think about selling immediately as she wanted to do, but to wait. Decisions made in a period of mourning, Violet said, were not necessarily the wisest. Advice was followed with a hard fact: that Cherryhill in actuality was not Susannah's to sell, that it belonged to her son, and Susannah was only one of four trustees. She did not profit from Mike's will. Almost everything was tied up in trusts for the child. Of the accident itself they did not speak, till the day Susannah telephoned concerning the snoopy reporter. And Violet said, "I know that man. He was an old acquaintance of my husband's. I believe I'll have him to tea."

What transpired between Violet and the tough reporter Susannah never knew. But he dropped the story and was heard saying in "21," when someone asked him what had happened to that piece he was going to write about the Brownes, that obviously the death was a tragic accident, and those poor women, the mother and the widow, had suffered sufficiently.

Soon afterward, Susannah took Rick out of kindergarten and the two of them went traveling, south to the Caribbean first, then to Europe, a moving, hurtling, restless sightseeing trip no child of six should have been able to tolerate, but somehow in a vagabond way they managed (though she found, in order to manage, it was necessary to go back to real drinks; to carry at all times a flask, just in case). And so she postponed reality for some months, not returning to Cherryhill till midsummer, when everyone she knew was away, at which point she immediately began occupying herself with the business of lawyers, the fight to sell the place.

Chapter Twenty-six

Then one morning, about eight months after Mike Browne died, Susannah woke up and realized he was dead, knew she had killed him.

"I didn't know it before," she said aloud to an empty bedroom. "I didn't know it before," she said aloud, in various rooms and expanses of Cherryhill, over subsequent days, until the afternoon she said it in a lavish bathroom-dressing room, to a wall of photographs, chronicle of a marriage.

They were all cleverly mounted on blocks of wood, without glass. She'd had them done for their ninth anniversary. There was Kitty's wedding picture, record of their beginning. There was a picture of the two of them at El Morocco, taken sometime during their courtship, a ghastly wild-eyed open-mouthed night club photograph. There were pictures of their own wedding and rather fuzzy blowups of ones they'd taken of each other on their honeymoon. There was a Cecil Beaton portrait of her that had appeared in *Vogue* and the *Life* cover picture. There was a Bachrach portrait of Mike at his desk, also a Toni Frissell of the two of them outdoors. There was a picture of Mike planting a flag on a mountain, of the two of them in a rubber pontoon, shooting the rapids of some wild river. There were records of their attendance at theater openings, costume balls, pictures of the old apartment, of a yacht. There was a classic neo-Edwardian family portrait, fifty people, taken on the occasion of Jimmy Browne's sixtieth birthday. There were many pictures acknowledging the advent of their son, his transformation from baby to boy. The very last of these was of his fifth birthday party, children in hats, streamers, blowers, confusion, Mike and Susannah behind their child, caught smiling proudly at the moment the birthday boy made his wish and blew out the candles.

That day, in Mike's dressing room, untouched since his death because she couldn't bear to go into the closet, or have anyone else go in, she took all the pictures off the wall and scattered them on the rug, and with a pair of scissors and a box of crayons Rick had left in her room, she went to work.

Sometime later Rick found her, but was not alarmed at first by the strange doodlings and the vicious slashes, which were not unlike the sort of mayhem he might create, given half a chance. He stood behind her blowing bubbles, only surprised, perhaps, that she didn't tell him to stop doing that indoors because the burst bubbles left a discoloring drip on the carpet.

So, having watched her put beards and mustaches on a Christmas grouping of Brownes and Kings, he saw her turn now to another group, the wedding party. She took the scissors and made little holes and gashes in certain figures, sketched in pen some obscene annotations and then with a yellow crayon she drew halos and angel wings on some, smiling at her handiwork, smiling at the fascinated little boy who finally asked her what she was doing.

"Playing," she said.

"Why are they angels?" he asked.

"Because they're dead."

"I understand. They're in heaven like my daddy."

"No. They're dead."

"That's what I *said*. And they've gone to heaven."

"No." She looked at him, so trusting and eager for knowledge, a small, fractured reflection of her, except for the blue eyes, which were, exactly, his father's. "That's not dead. That's just a story. Dead is like this."

She took the bubble maker from him and carefully blew a perfect globe, larger than any he had done, and released it. For a moment the bubble floated till it landed on the edge of a table and burst.

"That's dead," she said, pointing to nothingness.

Then the little boy began crying, ran out of the room crying and hollering, and she just sat there.

That night she went through the house breaking things—mirrors, china, slashing at curtains and furniture—and managed to do quite a bit of damage before Rick's new nurse and a maid found her, near dawn, and forcibly held her while someone else called a doctor and the grandmother. Presently a gray-haired woman came with an ambulance and some orderlies to take away the woman who had gone berserk, and later in the day a much younger woman came to collect the child and the nurse. Soon there was no one in the house but a caretaker.

And then there was no caretaker, only wreckers' trucks in the driveway and a big sign that read:

THE FUTURE SITE OF EXECUTIVE HILLS
A NEW WAY OF LIVING
HOMES FOR THE DISCRIMINATING.

Then followed sixteen years.

Of those years, Susannah Browne spent six, on and off, in mental hospitals and drying-out institutions, emerging for the last time in the early sixties cured. She had aged, but was sane and sober and more or less together. Returning to life, she moved to a new setting where no one knew her; a small quiet island in Long Island Sound. A year or so later she made a curious but sensible gesture. She changed her name. Or rather she returned herself to the character she had once been: Susan Rose, origins unknown, profession writer.

As for other members of the wedding party, life had gone beyond the obscene scrawls with which the deranged widow had disfigured their faces and bodies. In a single decade, already canceled out by death, left to right, had been: top row, Jay Lawrence, Lily Welles, Gus Gladstone, Peter Plainfield; bottom row, Mike Browne and Willis Metcalf.

Added to these, in the next eight years, were two more deaths, violent, sudden, the victims not yet forty—those of Diana Koenig and Kitty Jones.

Three years after Mike Browne's death, swimming off Eleuthera, Diana Koenig, formerly Diana Weatherby, born Diana Fayne, was drowned, leaving behind a sorrowing husband and three children by her former marriage. It seemed a cruel jest, this accident, striking her down when she seemed so happy in her new peaceful life. Except was she all that happy, a few cynics wondered, in her marriage to the brilliant, boring State Department man, leading the life of a suburban Washington housewife? Had she ever, really, gotten over Mike Browne? And if she were all that happy, what was she doing in the Bahamas without her husband, back with some of the old gang? What was she doing trying to swim to that coral reef against a powerful current?

Then, in the winter of 1964, the bride herself was gone.

In Rome, after a brief bout of pneumonia, Kitty St. John Jones, loveliest girl of her generation, at the age of thirty-seven, died in a hospital, only a few weeks after finally meeting the man she said she'd been looking for all her life. A great new man—so she wrote to Susannah Browne in a posthumously received letter—an internationally known photographer who had persuaded Kitty to marry him, give up her wandering expatriate life, and move back to New York where she belonged. Through everything, those two glamorous derelicts, Kitty Jones and Susannah Browne, had kept up by mail and transatlantic phone and occasional visits. When Kitty died, twenty years seemed totally wiped out.

That was the moment when Susannah, settled finally in her new anonymous island life, decided to resume the name of Susan Rose, as if Susannah Browne had never existed—and as if there were no issue, no flesh-and-blood son growing up in the custody of an aunt and uncle on the other side of the ocean.

Chapter Twenty-seven

"This boy who's coming," her lover said to Susan Rose. "How long since you've seen him?"

A pause. It was difficult to contemplate. "Almost ten years. Mike's sister Puss got custody. But I was judged well enough, ten summers ago, for him to visit me. I had a beach house on the South Shore. I was still trying, for the boy's sake, to be Mrs. Michael Browne." Nervously she ran her hands through her hair, short now, a tumbling, curling cap that hid a multitude of furrows and gouges, but still thick, undyed, only a few silver wires springing up. "I don't remember much about Rick. Brooding. An eleven-year-old Brando, never washed, never changed his clothes, treated me like something *unpardonable,* though never said anything, not one word about his father or his father's death, only asked for things to eat or the paper so he could look up the TV listings. No connection with that little boy I'd adored. I began drinking again, doing stupid things. Really dangerous things. After that there were no more visits, and Puss and George moved to London."

Another pause. Then, her voice rising as it had all her life, "What is he going to *look* like?" she asked. "What am I going to *say*?"

"You'll know when you see him." He handed her a cigarette, lit it, then, looking at his watch, a gesture she hated, said: "He should be here pretty soon. I'm going to sleep on the boat."

"Why? Why should you go? You're part of me." Her eyes flashed. There were still green lights in those eyes. The face might be drawn but the eyes were magnificent—thickly lashed, yearning, intense, occasionally lighting up with amusement. Eyes that had lured this man. "You're part of what he's coming to see."

They'd met walking on the beach, a month or so earlier, one foggy Saturday. He emerged from the mist with a big dog and asked to look at what she was collecting. "What's so special about broken glass?" he asked, examining the bits of blue and green and purple in her hand. He was big, ruddy-faced, and grizzled, expensively dressed in flannels and cashmere, though his knobby feet were bare.

"It pleases me," she said. "I fill jars with it. What would you pick up on a beach?"

"A girl," he said. Not likely, she thought; a rich fag, but she was wrong. A widower, a family man with grown-up children, that's what he turned out to be, and had found her again, later that same day, at a small party at the house of an elderly musician and had introduced himself. He had a flat-edged middle western name—Marcus Dillon; and a flat-edged middle western business, highly lucrative, totally devoid of glamour, that brought him east part of every year. He was intelligent, thoughtful, capable, and he'd reacted to Susan Rose, vivid, enigmatic, and beautifully turned out, as if she were Greta

Garbo. Later that weekend he had taken her on his chartered boat and made love to her, many times, more times than a middle-aged man usually makes love to a middle-aged woman, or a middle-aged woman desires to be made love to, and gave her back a piece of her identity.

She was thinking of marrying him.

"You know me. I'm stuffy about some things," he said. "Besides, this is one you have to handle alone. I'll come around in the morning." In the guest room off the living room, he threw a few things into a duffel bag.

"Oh, go ahead," she said, as if she could stop him, and threw at him a limp piece of Hershey bar, left over from earlier in the day—a symbol of descent, she thought ruefully. Once she had hurled Steuben and Lowestoft, now a Hershey bar.

In her dream the doorbell rang. She got out of bed, sun steaming around her, bay windows colored like stained glass, the bay windows of her old bachelor apartment. It kept ringing as she went toward the door. "Coming, coming," she said in the dream, "hold on," flinging the door open, and Mick stood there, only he didn't look like Mick, and he kept his hand on the bell, which kept ringing . . .

Half awake, she heard the door chime and didn't know where she was and said, "Who is it?" going toward the big heavy door. "Who is it?"

"It's me," said a voice. "Rick."

"God, Rick, I must have fallen asleep."

She opened the door. Mick stood there, only he didn't look like Mick, not quite. He was taller than Mick, younger than Mick, and his dark hair was shoulder length and he had a mustache. Neither of them knew what to do so they continued to stand in the doorway. "What time is it?" she asked.

"Late. After three."

"What happened? Come in, come in. Do you have a bag?"

"Just this." He was carrying a big bookstore shopping bag, full as a Christmas stocking, with clothes, objects.

"I was late starting. Then I got lost. Really lost. I guess I was nervous. I don't usually get lost."

"How'd you get across? The last ferry, even Saturday night, is two."

"Well . . . I pulled a little something . . ." He was looking at her very intently, but kindly, openly, frowning slightly. His brows were dark, like wings. She noticed the polished boots, the jeans, the light, faintly striped shirt, open at the neck, the dark vest. She thought how beautiful his neck was. A confusion of images assaulted her: image of the vest, navy blue, part of some dress suit, funeral suit, wedding suit, image of another young man taking off his coat, pulling off his tie, standing before her in his elegant vest exposing a beautiful, vulnerable boy's neck . . . image of a neck . . . image of the jeans, an eleven-year-old boy, long legs in jeans, next to a woman, herself, fallen drunkenly to the floor . . . image of a face, Mick's face, under the disguise of long hair and mustache, Mick in wig and mustache and pirate's costume at a masked ball . . .

"Oh, my dear," she said, "my dear, dear boy, please don't be nervous. I'm glad you pulled a little something. That must have been an expensive little something at this hour of the night. I'm sorry, I'm going to cry . . ." Overwhelmed by a sense of lost years, and not caring whether she should or shouldn't, whether it was his lead or hers, she put her arms around him, felt his arms closing around her, buried her face for a minute in his shoulder, and sobbed.

Chapter Twenty-eight

She awoke to dazzling nine o'clock sunshine and the sound through her closed bedroom door of disturbing, familiar music. Quickly, she washed and dressed, water drowning out whatever it was about that beat that disturbed her.

So good-by dear and amen . . . opening the door she heard someone singing to a piano. *Here's hoping we'll meet now and then* . . . For a moment she had a sense of dropping through a trap door. She didn't know where she was. Then she saw her son flopped in the chair next to the record player. He was barefoot, rumpled, and alive and bright as the morning. "Hi," he said, putting down the magazine he had been reading. "I was hoping you'd wake up soon." His morning smile was shy and sleepy. "If you hadn't woken up soon I was going to bang on your door." The smile broadened, almost into the full grin.

"What's that on the record player?" she asked sharply.

"A present for you. I hope you don't have it."

She looked at the jacket: she knew the voice and the song, both favorites of Mike Browne's. It was music she had carefully avoided. "No, I don't have it," she said.

I get no kick from champagne! Mere alcohol doesn't thrill me at all . . . The songs went through her like sharp needles.

"Have you had breakfast?" the woman asked the boy.

"Long ago. There's coffee made."

In the kitchen the music pursued her. She began wondering if there was an edge to her son's casual gift; if he sensed the connection between those songs and her life with his father and was trying in some way to test her.

"Rick?" She leaned across the counter that divided kitchen from the dining portion of the living room. "That's not the greatest for me, that record," she said lightly. "Those songs. You here. It's too much."

"I'm sorry," he said. "Someone thought you'd like it. They said all the mothers were buying this record. There's something about it that makes me feel good."

"When you were very little, sometimes, when we were having a big party, before the guests came you'd listen to the pianist warming up . . ."

"This guy?"

"Someone just like him."

"Why didn't you ever come to get me?" he asked suddenly, turning off the record player, crossing the room toward her, and sitting on one of the high wooden stools that faced the counter.

"I wasn't well. I wasn't safe. You should remember that awful summer."

"I was a little punk. And you were sick. But afterward why didn't you come to get me?"

"I didn't know you wanted me to." She felt tears coming again. The effort to control herself was torture. But she sensed tears, which had been the only possible response the night before, were not suited to the morning. Refilling her cup, she sat in the sun at the kitchen table. He came and sat with her.

"That's super coffee," she said. "How does a college boy come to make such good coffee—in England," and chatted inconsequentially about coffee making, expounding on brands and pots, from there moving onto the subject of food in general, explaining the wonders of this kitchen she'd designed herself, having suddenly become a cook in middle age, turning on her special brand of phony merriment. She was overwhelmed with the feeling that she couldn't face this boy-man who looked so much like that other boy-man who used to teeter on his chair just as this one was doing, preparing to cut through her idle chatter and pounce.

So, suddenly, "Mother," he said. "I want to talk to you about something. I want to talk to you about my father."

"I don't know if I can . . ." fixing on him big pleading eyes.

"I want to talk about the day he died. I want to talk about that right away and then afterward we can relax."

"You're very impatient."

"I came to tell you something."

A noise from her, not quite interpretable, of protest, pain.

"Listen: a month ago at a party in London, I met a woman named Natalie," he began. "American. Married to an Englishman, Lord Buford. She knew you and my father. She didn't know if you'd remember her. Her name was Natalie Jones."

"Don't teeter. You'll break the chair. I remember her." Eyes no longer pleading, but gelid, green glacial water.

"Don't ice over. *He loved you.*"

They had met, Rick said, he and Natalie, Lady Buford, at a large after-theater party in a house on Eaton Square, a typical mixture, he said, of titles, talents, and kids, including the model who'd brought him. Early in the evening he'd noticed a blonde staring at him as if she knew him. Finally, she had come over to him and asked, "Are you Mike Browne's son?" She had a whispering, beckoning voice and an arresting face—tanned skin, dark, swimming eyes—framed by a halo of blonde baby hair: an older woman on the prowl, he decided. "She said she knew Father, and that I looked just like him, only taller." Rick's voice was light and amused. The expression on Susan's face, however, was not remotely one of amusement. "Then she said that Father would have thought my mustache was silly," he continued. "She wanted to know everything about me. I told her I was at Oxford, had no future plans, that sort of thing. She kept staring at me and when I asked her why, she said she felt as if she were talking to a ghost. Pretty soon an old walrus, her husband, removed her, saying there was someone he wanted her to meet, but later I found her again and asked her to lunch."

"Honestly, Rick"—Susan poured herself more coffee—"I don't see . . . . Can you get to the point? Your father got to the point of a story very fast."

"I have to tell it my way. Am I boring you?"

"No."

A day or so later, he went on, they met in one of those cheap Italian restaurants where the lighting is murky, the food authentic. "We discovered we were both a couple of spaghetti pigs," he said. His mother didn't smile. "I asked Natalie to tell me about my father, if she was one of his girl friends. She said she'd always known Brownie—that's what she called him."

"That's what everybody called him," Susan said. "Except me."

"The first time she really noticed him, she said, was at her brother's wedding. Even at eight she realized he was beautiful, though not very polite. He kept calling her 'kid.' Apparently you, Mother, were the big girl who chased her away."

"Not far enough," said Susan. "Go on."

"You see, I was always told that at the time of his death, Father was about to leave you."

"Were you?" Susan's voice was level, her expression stony. "By whom? Your Aunt Puss?"

Ignoring the interruption, he went on. "But Natalie said, 'Your father wasn't going to leave your mother for anyone. Not even me and God knows I was younger and prettier and more determined than most.'"

"Look," Susan said, "I don't believe I can sit and listen to any more of this."

"Hold on," said her son. "It's because of Natalie and what she told me that I'm here. I wasn't about to come and visit you —ever. I believed you had killed Father on purpose because of some other woman. Aunt Puss and Uncle George believed you had. So did Gran, or at least that's what Aunt Puss said. It's not pleasant being brought up thinking your mother is an evil woman. Don't be too hard on Natalie. She gave you back your son. I know now you had no reason to kill him."

Susan was frozen dumb, watching Rick's flushed face.

At that moment Marcus Dillon appeared.

Rick Browne assumed an expression of annoyance so like his father's Susan wanted to laugh and to cry at the same time. How could he be so much like him when he'd never known him?

"Hey, Marc, come in, we're in here." Her voice was high-pitched, fakey, and relieved. The boy looked at her resentfully.

There were introductions, some attempts on Susan's part and Marcus's at pleasantries, an offer of coffee refused. "Am I interrupting something?" Marc asked, looking at them in his kindly, quizzical fashion, putting his hand on Susan's head, gently pulling her hair, to let the boy know this wasn't just some casual neighbor dropping by to be dismissed.

"Heavens, no," said Susan. The boy remained silent, watching.

"How about coming for a sail?" Marcus asked. "The wind's perfect."

"That would be lovely," Susan said. "I'll make sandwiches. I have some salmon left from last night and some cucumbers and cheese. I'll boil some eggs . . . how about it, Rick?"

The boy hesitated, but only for a minute, "I think, if you don't mind, sir," he said to the older man, "I'd like to be alone with my mother, for awhile anyhow. We were talking." He was neither rude nor polite, just very matter-of-fact.

The woman said nothing.

"Of course," said Marcus Dillon. "Come by late this afternoon, if you want. We'll have a drink and watch the sunset." He, too, was matter-of-fact, neither rude nor polite, apparently undisturbed—a nice-looking open-faced man with good legs and too much stomach, handling with perfect presence an ungracious boy who hadn't even stood up when he came in, a boy who looked more like a pirate or a rock star than a young man who has just come into a fortune of twenty million, with twenty more to come.

Now that the man was going, though, the boy pulled out his fabulous white smile: his father's smile when he was dismissing someone, yet still wanted to keep the person on a string.

"You didn't have to be so rude," Susan said to her son.

"I wasn't rude. I was frank. He understood. Is that your boyfriend?" A real smile now.

"Never mind. And look, I don't know that I want to hear any further messages from Natalie Jones."

"I promise you do," Rick said, proceeding with Natalie's story.

Years went by, Natalie had told Rick, when she didn't see the Brownes, camp years, school years, the years in which she grew up. They met again, she, Mike, and Susannah, at a New Year's party at her brother's. She was still in school, but everyone, including Mike Browne, mistook her for a twenty-year-old. "She said she fell in love that night with both of you," Rick went on. "I guess a lot of people did. She said, 'There was something electric about them. They were both so dark and exotic and stylish, and always up to no good. Wherever they were, things happened. Except sooner or later,' she had added, 'if you're a grownup normal girl and you fall in love with a couple, you sort things out and begin concentrating on the man.'

"So she concentrated, and kept concentrating, without much luck, she admitted, for more than a year. Till one afternoon in the early summer of 1956 she ran into Father on the street and they had a drink together. You were away in Europe, Natalie was occupying her parents' empty apartment"—a gesture indicated the rest—"She told me she was crazy about him so she just assumed he was crazy about her—and was very philosophical when he left to join you, Mother, a week or so later, to go cruising down the Turkish coast."

"What are you trying to prove?" Susan Rose asked her son. "What was she trying to say?"

"I'm almost through."

"And what were you doing, you fool boy, all the while she was telling you about her love affair with your father?"

"Eating an excellent lunch."

"And falling in love with her yourself."

"Are you kidding? That's sick. I have a girl.

"When Father got back from Europe," Rick continued doggedly, "Natalie expected to see him right away, but he didn't come around or call or anything. When she ran into him at a party, it was like the whole thing had never happened. Then the day of the night Father was killed he walked into the jewelry store where Natalie worked and she thought she had him back. He'd come, he said, to get you a really worthwhile Christmas present, but there were other jewelry stores in New York."

"She's a liar," said Susan. "So was he."

"Listen . . ." But he didn't have to order her. He had her now, she couldn't have moved if she'd tried.

"He wanted to get you a ring. A star sapphire. Natalie thought it old-fashioned, not chic. She told him, 'Get her a ruby. Red's Susannah's color.' He said it was to replace one you'd lost years earlier. It seemed to be some sort of private joke. He wanted to have the inside engraved: *Found in the East River*. He wanted it in time for Christmas. Natalie said, 'You're out of luck.' 'Arrange it,' Father said, 'and I'll take you to lunch.'

"It was a gay lunch and after a couple of drinks Natalie got up enough courage to bring up the summer. And then he said, 'I owe you an apology for not being straight with you.' She knew: something desperately *boring* was coming.

"'I suppose you fell in love on that cruise with some other girl,' she said. And he said, 'Other girls aren't the problem, old dear. The problem is Susannah. In Europe, I started up an old love affair with my wife. I always do.' Natalie realized it was no go—that he was all yours." Rick smiled, looking almost tenderly at the impassive woman facing him. "She said you and Father were one of the great love affairs of the century. She said, 'Susannah could no more have murdered Mike Browne than she could have killed herself. I *know*.'

"The next morning, though," Rick finished, "when she heard the news, Natalie canceled the order for the ring. She was never quite sure whether she did this out of anger, because whether you meant to or not, you had caused the death of the man she adored, or out of kindness—some misguided notion of sparing you hurt. Afterward she had realized she'd wiped out the last evidence of his love."

"On that drive home," Rick asked his mother, "didn't you *know* how he felt, didn't he tell you, stop worrying about other women, that he loved you . . . ?"

"It's too dim and long ago," she said. "I can't remember anymore." He was a sentimental boy, after all, she thought; his father's son. "Revelations, revelations, they're a trick." She stood up. "I'm going to make us some lunch," she said. And then, "Do you think you've brought me some sort of good news, you silly boy? Silly, presumptuous boy."

But he kept looking at her so steadily, with such trust, as if, in spite of everything, he was ready to love her in the simplest, easiest way, that she had to turn away, knowing nothing was simple or easy.

Chapter Twenty-nine

A few mornings later Rick Browne received a telephone call and told his mother they were going into New York.

"You're bossy," she said. "That's something I've learned about you. Supposing I don't want to go into New York. It's too lovely here."

"It'll be lovely in the city."

"Was there something special you wanted to do?"

"There's someone special I want you to meet."

"Oh?"

"The girl I'm driving across the country with."

"Girl?"

"Of course, girl. What do you think? This is 1972, mother."

"Right, right. I don't know what I'm going to wear. I have

nothing to wear into town this time of year. I feel like a *hick*."

"I've seen your closets. You're set to go round the world."

She could say she had nothing to wear, but when she stepped out of the house an hour later she was perfect: casually dressed in pale colors, right out of the latest *Vogue*, the only brightness a silk scarf tied around her head and violet glasses, equipment for a fast drive in an open car. "This girl," her son said, looking at her in frank admiration and amusement, "you won't scare her, like you imagine you are going to. She'll just think you're spectacular."

"You think you know me after four days?" Also amused.

They were happy together, mother and son, at the beginning of that drive, joking, teasing.

Some minutes before the boy at the wheel spoke, before they reached that particular exit, the woman began getting nervous, talking a great deal and rather charmingly, intending to ward off the question that he asked anyhow: "Somewhere around here we'd get off, wouldn't we, to go to Cherryhill?"

"There wasn't an expressway then."

"No, but somewhere soon there's an exit off this expressway that would take us there."

"There is no Cherryhill. There's something called, I believe, Executive Hills."

"It would be the next exit, Blue Hollow Road, that's the one Cherryhill gave onto."

"Rick!"

"I want to."

"I don't."

"Have you never?"

"Never. You do it sometime without me. With your girl."

"No point to that."

"*Now* where do you turn?"

"At the next corner, left I think, wait, there's a bit of the old fence." Maybe it would be all right.

"I remember that. It went all the way around the property. I remember a lot, you know. When I was three, four, five. For years I had dreams about this place." Past the dairy farm, and the deserted army training post with the "Keep Out" sign, and a stretch of unkempt shrubbery, and loops of old, rusty wire fencing. Then the shrubbery began to gleam and glisten. A low brick wall appeared leading to two thick white-brick pillars connected by a high iron arch from which hung a scalloped sign:

EXECUTIVE HILLS
A CONCEPT IN LIVING
PRIVATE. RESIDENTS AND THEIR GUESTS ONLY.

"Was this the main entrance?" the boy asked.

"It can't be. It must be the lower end of the property that used to be lovely woods. Now look at it." She laughed a mirthless laugh.

The road forked immediately inside the gates and forked again. And there, where there used to be the only remaining cowslips, dog-toothed violets, wild buttercups and spring beauties on Long Island, there where once she and Mike Browne had walked over fallen logs, through *allées* of birches, where along snaking paths he had led Rick on a pony, there were manicured lawns and houses, house after house climbing up the side of the hill. Houses that seemed small at first glance, but when you looked closer grew larger.

There were lanais, breezeways, three-car garages, weather vanes of elaborate design, details that would have suited the grand mansions of an earlier era reduced and combined cunningly into houses that were neither small nor large, neither all Colonial, Tudor, Mediterranean, Palladian, nor Mussolini Modern, neither all wood nor brick nor stone nor shingle, neither all gabled nor turreted nor porticoed, rather a bland mixture of everything. The yards were meticulous, with beautifully kept evergreens and rhododendrons and only a few flowers. But there was no one in them. All the terraces, cantilevered and cut from the hillsides with such cleverness and expense were empty of humans. Only an occasional car as shiny and new as the houses and lawns sat in a driveway.

"It's not that early," Rick said, as the road wound slowly up the hill. "Do you suppose they're all dead. Shall I honk? I think I'll sing."

"No. They're in their houses. Outdoors is dangerous."

"It's incredible. I've never believed America was as rich as they say it is. New York is a mess. Even Park and Fifth look sort of run down and seedy. But this . . ."

"It's horrible," said Susan, her face drawn, looking suddenly very old beside him. It wasn't going to be all right. Not in any way.

"Snob." Still trying to keep it light, touristy.

"Where are we? There isn't a tree I can place. I'd say that's where the greenhouses were, but where is the row of apple trees that went down to them. And the stables should have been down there. You'd have thought someone would have wanted to save an elm. Or at least one of the cherry trees. Do you see anything that resembles a cherry tree?"

"Don't get upset," Rick said. "This is life." So they turned off Hemlock St., onto Elm, off Elm onto Locust and off Locust onto Cherry, which kept on climbing, without passing one of Violet's trees, which gave the streets and lanes and circles their names.

"They got *rid* of the cherries," she said, her heart beating very fast, as Cherry Avenue turned into Cherry Lane and then into Cherry Circle and they seemed to be reaching the highest point of the land where the house had been, and then suddenly they found themselves going down again. "They even got rid of the view. That was the greatest view on Long Island and you can't see a thing for all those evergreens. And the house and the terrace and the lawn and the balustrades. And the beautiful women and the beautiful men . . . *why* did you bring me here . . . ?"

"Come on, mother," Rick suddenly was impatient. "I wanted to see. These are my roots. But you know and I know, beautiful or not, they were a bunch of bastards. They couldn't have hung on a moment longer than they did. They had to go. The only reason you're still around is that you were never one of them."

"Let's get out of here," Susan said. "Let's get out of here as quickly as possible."

"Don't turn right, turn left. This isn't the way we came." She was now giving directions in a thin, imperative voice. "Now right, turn right . . ." It was a maze, a torturing, confusing maze, at its center the minotaur called memory.

He did what he was told and became hopelessly lost. It was impossible to tell the difference between the way they'd come and the way they were going. The streets were named for birds instead of trees—Goldfinch and Cardinal, Bob White and Tanager. "Keep going downhill. We've got to get out somewhere. This can't go on forever." There was hysteria in her voice as she tried to laugh. "The whole world hasn't become Executive Hills."

Then she saw the gate.

Directly in front of them, with a couple of honest-to-goodness locust trees on either side, at the edge of all this manicured counterfeit was the gate, rusted iron set in huge stones, with the tangled initials still at its heart, although the gold had gone. It was closed and would never open again. Piled on either side was the residue of the builders, broken tiles, plasterers' rubble, a pile of bricks.

"Damn," Rick said. "This is ridiculous. We've hit a dead

end." Then he saw his mother's face. He, too, realized where they were.

"Stop the car a minute," she said. She tried to light a cigarette, but her hands were shaking too badly. He lit it for her, placed it between her lips.

"God, I'm selfish," he said. "I thought coming here together would . . . I don't know, I thought you'd *say* something about what I said, *say* something about my father. I've been waiting three days."

"It's all right," she said. "But that story you told me, what you thought it meant, it doesn't."

"She doesn't lie. Natalie is one person who never lies."

"I'm not saying she lied. I lied. Always."

"There's something you ought to know about your father and me," Susan Rose said to her son, facing the minotaur, memory, in the guise of a rusty piece of ironwork, a gate beside which a man had died. "The night he died, I told him I wanted to leave him. Natalie Jones had nothing to do with it, one way or the other. She was peanuts. I'd asked him for a divorce."

"That's not possible," said her son.

"I told another version of that night so many times I came almost to believe it myself. The speculation was: had I meant to kill him because I loved him so much and was obsessed with the fear of losing him? *If* I had meant to kill him, Rick, *if* it was a loaded accident, so to speak, it was because *I* wanted *out*. If that had been known, there would have been a lot more questions. Do you understand?"

"No."

"I'd had enough of him and his wandering eye and petty affairs. Now I'm telling you, so you'll know. I wasn't a poor pitiable creature. I wasn't terrified of losing him. I wanted to marry someone else. And your father couldn't stand that. He would have fought me to the end."

"Who? Who did you want to marry?"

"That cruise Natalie mentioned. Your father thought he was recommencing an old affair with me. He always recommenced an affair with me when someone else found me attractive. Well, I was commencing a new and very serious affair myself with Sasha Garden, whose boat we were on. You've heard of Sasha Garden, haven't you?"

Rick's face told her he had, told her more but it was too late to stop. Too late to reconsider the wisdom of correcting that last patronizing misrepresentation her beautiful high-born husband had left behind: That somehow, even beyond death, he was calling the shots.

"I wanted to marry Sasha Garden," she said, "and he wanted very much to marry me."

Mike Browne, that sure is a big jump up from me, Bill Wolfe had said to her long ago. *But who's going to be a step up from Mike Browne? Those people own half of New York.* Sasha Garden, that was who was a step up from Mike Browne. In the ghastly silence now filling the car, she thought for a moment about Sasha. She hadn't thought about him in ages. Robert Alexander Garden, who appeared to own half the world, and who could have bought Mike Browne in the morning and sold him the same afternoon. Indeed Sasha had once offered to do just that for Susannah, to help her get some of her own back.

"Darling, would you like to see that cocky husband of yours squirm a little?" Sasha had asked her one brilliant Mediterranean day, standing at the tiller of his yacht, bronzed as an Indian, flashing his Cheshire cat grin, watching Mike turning on the charm for some other guest. "Would that amuse you, dearest?"

"Let me get my divorce first," she'd replied. "That's going to take a bit of maneuvering. Then you can do what you please."

"I did indeed carry on about Natalie that afternoon," Susan Rose said now to her son, who was no longer looking at her. "I pounced on the name as I had pounced many times in the past. But it was a performance."

Natalie was the excuse she had been searching for since summer. She would pretend Natalie was the last straw when in actuality she was happy that Mike would have Natalie to comfort him. "Also," Susan said to the statue, Rick, beside her, "I was delighted that Mike would remove Natalie from the table of my beloved Sasha where, as far as I was concerned, she dined entirely too frequently."

The presence of Natalie Jones gave Susannah courage to do what she had been wanting to do for months. She had not meant to tell Mike till after Christmas, but she announced to him that very afternoon, December 21, shortest day of the year, that she wanted a divorce.

"That was what we were fighting about," Susan Rose said to her son. "That was the reason for the ashtray. Remember the ashes he dumped in the tub, Rick? You thought it was a joke."

Rick said nothing, and would say nothing until she had finished. He stared straight ahead, through the windshield, at the ruined gate.

Immediately, Susan continued, Mike had asked her if there was someone else.

"No one," she lied, without hesitation, believing herself smarter than he, knowing she and Sasha Garden had been perfectly discreet, not like Mike and Diana Weatherby, long ago.

Mike had let it pass. He said, simply, "Natalie is nothing. No one has ever been anything except you."

"I don't even care enough anymore to tell you I don't believe you," she said. "I meant what I said."

"You don't mean it," he said. "You're my girl. You're tired, that's all. You have a cold. Christmas is always a bitch. So cut the act and get your bath or we'll be late."

"It's not an act," she'd screamed as Nanny and Rick entered. *"I've had it with you."*

There had been the bathtub scene, as reported, with the ashtray dumped in the tub. There had been the front hall scene, the car scene, the dinner party scene, everything as she'd always reported it, only not quite.

Driving home, however, in the record-breaking cold, there had not been silence. She told him again: she wanted her freedom. He laughed at her. But he was in a nastier mood; he was also drunk. He continued to dismiss her. "I love you," he said. "I'd never let you go."

And then, at the moment she stopped the car in front of the gate, Mike turned to Susannah and said: "That guy you think you're in love with. Six months of each other and you would both be slashed to ribbons. He's a barracuda and so are you. You think marriage is a jail with me. Wait till he gives you his boots to shine. Six months later he'll have a mistress. You don't like that kind of stuff. Actually, I doubt he'll marry you. Because not married to me, divorced by me, you are *nothing.* He might marry Natalie Jones. But Susannah Browne, formerly Susan Rose, formerly Susannah Rosoff? Don't kid yourself."

"What are you talking about?"

"You think I don't know what's been going on?" he said, getting out of the car. "You think I'm that dumb?"

His words filled her with an anger she had never experienced before, a desire to obliterate him from the face of the earth.

In such spirit did she start up the car.

But still, she did scream all those things at his dying body about loving him. Yes, she did, because the instant he was gone she knew nothing mattered except the two of them and nothing would matter very much ever again.

"What I wrote on the card with the flowers," she said to her son, "was the truth. It's still the truth. I never got over him. Seeing you makes me realize that in a very bitter way. But I couldn't stand the way we were. I couldn't stand our marriage."

Backed off, backed out, free of the center, free of the maze, out of the nightmare past, once more awake in the present on a perfectly normal highway, Rick Browne asked Susan Rose, his mother: "Why have you told me this? It wasn't necessary to tell me this. I may not forgive you for telling me." His face was unreadable.

"I may not forgive you for telling me about Natalie. Or for bringing me here today."

"What happened to the guy? Mr. Garden? Why didn't you marry him?"

"Even Mr. Garden had some scruples and a distaste for scandal. Stealing Mike Browne's wife was one thing. But marrying the woman who killed him was another. Mr. Garden did me what good turns he could. He took care of everything at the time of the accident. And then one morning I woke up and he was gone. Remember that trip we took, the spring after your father died? I tried to go after Mr. Garden. But once that man was gone, he was gone. The following year he astonished everyone by marrying—not a movie star, not some young and glamorous member of the jet set—but an elegant middle-aged Boston bluestocking whose ancestors on both sides went back to Puritan times. Final respectability, I suppose. As far as I know he's still married to her."

On the road feeding into the expressway, Rick took the entrance marked Long Island East instead of Long Island West.

"That's not the way into New York," said Susan.

"I'm not taking you into New York. I'm taking you home," the boy said. And after a while: "So you meant to kill him after all. Aunt Puss and Gran had the right idea."

"I don't believe so. No, Rick," said his mother with great definiteness. "What I've told you doesn't mean it wasn't an accident, a horrible, ill-timed accident. It just means I wasn't the kind of pathetic, lost soul you and everybody else thought I was."

But from her son, knowing the truth of that last day, there would be no release, no more than there had been from Violet who perhaps, after all, had also known what was really going on between the Brownes—she who knew everything. No more than there had been from the Squad who had said from the start the Brownie and "that woman" would never make it.

In Susan's driveway, Rick stopped so suddenly the gravel sprayed. They both got out. It took him a minute to collect his few things.

"Won't you ever come back?" she asked.

"I may not be back in New York at all. If I am I'll try to call you."

"Don't judge me."

"Don't judge yourself."

"You're a hard boy, Rick. I thought you might be gentle and sweet."

"I'm your son."

"Yes," she said, and for the first time in many hours smiled, a seductive smile, sweet and gentle, shining out of a hard, tired face. "And the day you know that, really know it, you'll be back."

"Could be." Briefly he smiled, too, put his hands on her shoulders, let her memorize his dark face lit up by blue eyes and white teeth, allowed her to find in those blue eyes, which were Mike's eyes, and Violet's eyes, a pinpoint of hope.

Chapter Thirty

When the phone rang, Susan Rose and Marcus Dillon were sitting in her garden, enjoying the last of a fine May afternoon. Slumped in a canvas chair, chewing a pencil, she was editing some pages of typescript. He was reading, stretched out on a chaise longue. On the twentieth ring, he said to her impatiently, "Well, answer it."

"No, thanks."

The ringing continued. "Someone knows your bad habits," said Marc. "It might be important."

"What on earth could be important at six o'clock on a Saturday afternoon?"

"It might be for me. Did that ever occur to you? I'm expecting a call."

"Then answer it yourself."

They snapped at each other like an old married couple, though they weren't wed and never would be. She had been telling him that for eleven months now, ever since the visit of her son. "I don't want to be Mrs. Marcus Dillon," she kept saying in a variety of ways, but he didn't seem to care how determined she was. He loved her and he wanted to secure her and lately had been putting the pressure on. She, for her part, ignoring the pressure, simply went on writing, six or eight hours a day. Ever since the visit of her son, she had been working on a novel, a simple story, as Mike had once suggested, that any fool could understand, even that wretched son of hers—prudish, judgmental boy who'd come and gone and, cruelly, never sent so much as a postcard since.

"It's for you," Marc said, standing in the doorway.

"Who is it?"

"Your son."

"Hello, Rick." Have some pride, Susan Rose, she told herself, be cool and stern. Instead, "Where the hell *are* you?" she heard herself say, and "God, I'm glad to hear your voice." As Violet had long ago observed, pride is often beside the point.

"I'm in London, mother."

"Heavens! You sound around the corner. Are you coming to New York?"

"Maybe later. That's not why I called. I have something to tell you. I got married today."

"Good Lord," she said gaily, not too nervously. "I didn't think people your age got married anymore. Who's the poor girl?"

"Natalie Buford and I were married this afternoon."

Silence. Absolute silence.

"Hello . . . Hello . . . are you there?"

"I'm here. Is this some sort of joke?"

"No joke."

"I don't believe you," she said. The phone in her hand

seemed unbearably heavy. "What time is it there?" she asked foolishly.

"What does that have to do with anything? It's almost midnight."

"It's still afternoon here. It's a lovely afternoon. Is it a lovely evening there?"

"Yes. It's raining . . . come *on*, mother. I didn't want you to read about it in the papers."

"I thank you for that, Rick. It must have taken a certain amount of courage to make this call. I don't know what to say."

"Don't say anything. We just wanted you to know. You're the first person we've called. We're very happy."

"I'm glad you're happy, Rick. It's important. To be happy. I hope everything works out." Between nearly every word was a pause in which the self-control of Susan Rose reinstated itself.

"We'll be coming to New York in the fall," he said. "Maybe . . ." He hesitated.

"Maybe. Let's see." Then, just before she hung up a thought occurred to her that gave her pleasure. There was, after all, a bright side to everything. "God, Rick," she said, her voice lightening, "I'd give anything to see the expression on your Aunt Puss's face when you tell her."

"What was that all about?" asked Marcus Dillon when she came back outside.

"He's gone and married Natalie Buford. Natalie Buford's almost old enough to be his mother, for God's sake."

"You must be very upset. And angry."

"I don't believe it yet." She turned to look at him. He had just the right expression on his face, sympathy mixed with a skeptical inquiry. "*Fourteen years*. I had a friend who was fifteen years older than her husband. But they were both middle-aged."

"Poor Susan," he said, drawing her toward him. She let herself be comforted by him, thinking she could always put him back in his place later. "Listen to me," he said. "Your son is going to be fine. He's done something nutty and possibly quite disagreeable, but he's young and he has some brains. He'll survive. He's a survivor. Like you." He leaned over to kiss her and she didn't push him away.

"If you weren't here," she said, "you'd be the only person I'd try to get in touch with. Everyone else who might have something to say, whether cynical or wise or comforting, is dead. Violet . . . Kitty . . . Gus Gladstone . . . poor Jay Lawrence . . . Pete Plainfield . . . even awful old Diana. She'd have had fun with this one. God, what was *wrong* that day, who was that photographer anyhow? Who had the evil eye? Me, d'you suppose? I wore a red dress. Mike said you shouldn't wear a red dress to a wedding. Mike. Jesus, *Mike!* He'd disinherit the kid."

Mike . . . sixteen years dead . . . was so real to her at that moment she could see him, touch him, smell him. She could hear the angry mingling of their voices, his snooty prep school accent that had gone down in the world, her nasal tones that had climbed up quite a bit. He'd have threatened to cut Rick off, to lock up the trusts, and she would have had to stand up for the boy's right to determine his own life. That would have been some battle. For an instant she was Susannah Browne, wife of Mike Browne, and for just that instant she wished herself dead, not because she hated Mike, but because she wanted to be with him: to tell him about Rick, to hear him explode. Dear God, Mike would be almost fifty. Not possible. But yes he would. And certainly would raise hell at his wayward son.

Then the feeling passed. Susan Rose pulled herself together. She smiled at Marcus Dillon. She pretended her eyes were dry.

"I really have to laugh at that boy," she said. "'That's sick,' he said to me when I suggested he might be falling in love with Natalie. He's a chip off the old block." She made a small, exact noise: hmmph. "Well, Mike always said Natalie would marry above herself."

ABOUT THE AUTHOR

Mary Ellin Barrett was born in New York City and was graduated from Barnard College. She is the daughter of the composer Irving Berlin and the author Ellin Berlin. Her first novel, *Castle Ugly*, was published in 1966. Currently the book reviewer for *Cosmopolitan* magazine, Mrs. Barrett lives in New York with her children and her husband, the journalist Marvin Barrett.